So You Want to

Publish Your Own
BOOK & e-BOOK

A Step-by-Step Guide to Fun & Profitable Publishing

By Myra Faye Turner

Foreward By Beth Reekles

SO YOU WANT TO PUBLISH YOUR OWN BOOK & E-BOOK: A STEP-BY-STEP GUIDE TO FUN & PROFITABLE PUBLISHING

1405 SW 6th Avenue • Ocala, Florida 34471 • Phone 800-814-1132 • Fax 352-622-1875
Website: www.atlantic-pub.com • Email: sales@atlantic-pub.com
SAN Number: 268-1250

Library of Congress Cataloging-in-Publication Data

Names: Turner, Myra Faye, author.
Title: So you want to publish your own book & e-book: a step-by-step guide to fun & profitable publishing / by Myra Faye Turner.
Description: Ocala, Florida : Atlantic Publishing Group, Inc., [2017] | Includes bibliographical references and index.
Identifiers: LCCN 2017025350| ISBN 9781620232194 (alk. paper) | ISBN 1620232197 (alk. paper)
Subjects: LCSH: Authorship—Marketing. | Authorship. | Self-publishing. | Electronic publishing.
Classification: LCC PN161 .T87 2017 | DDC 808.02—dc23 LC record available at https://lccn.loc.gov/2017025350

Printed in the United States

PROJECT MANAGER: Lisa McGinnes • lmcginnes@atlantic-pub.com
INTERIOR LAYOUT: Nicole Sturk • nicolejonessturk@gmail.com

Reduce. Reuse.
RECYCLE.

A decade ago, Atlantic Publishing signed the Green Press Initiative. These guidelines promote environmentally friendly practices, such as using recycled stock and vegetable-based inks, avoiding waste, choosing energy-efficient resources, and promoting a no-pulping policy. We now use 100-percent recycled stock on all our books. The results: in one year, switching to post-consumer recycled stock saved 24 mature trees, 5,000 gallons of water, the equivalent of the total energy used for one home in a year, and the equivalent of the greenhouse gases from one car driven for a year.

Over the years, we have adopted a number of dogs from rescues and shelters. First there was Bear and after he passed, Ginger and Scout. Now, we have Kira, another rescue. They have brought immense joy and love not just into our lives, but into the lives of all who met them.

We want you to know a portion of the profits of this book will be donated in Bear, Ginger and Scout's memory to local animal shelters, parks, conservation organizations, and other individuals and nonprofit organizations in need of assistance.

– Douglas & Sherri Brown,
President & Vice-President of Atlantic Publishing

Table of Contents

Foreword...11

Introduction 15

How to Use This Guide.. 18

Chapter 1: Get Ready...23

Considerations on the Writing Life................................23

Can you handle rejection? 24

Why your manuscript may get rejected 26

Can you handle success? 27

Can you take constructive criticism? 29

Do you have the skills to write–or can you learn?.................... 29

Can you stick to a writing routine? 31

Can you meet deadlines? 32

Can you keep writing in the face of adversity? 33

Do you need a dedicated workspace? 34

How Will You Publish?..35

Chapter 2: Get Set 37

Choosing Your Genre 38

Fiction...38

Romance.. 38

Horror *39*

Thriller/Suspense *39*

Science Fiction *40*

Fantasy *41*

Mystery/Crime *41*

Action-Adventure *42*

Historical *42*

Young Adult *43*

Nonfiction 46

How-to *48*

Self-Help *48*

Travel Guides *49*

Cooking and Food *49*

Humor *50*

Creative Nonfiction 51

Adventure *51*

Travelogues *51*

Biography *51*

Memoir *52*

True Crime *53*

Essays *53*

Sharpening Your Writing Skills 54

Writing Classes & Workshops 54

Writing Groups 56

How to evaluate a writing group *58*

Keeping a Writer's Notebook or Journal 60

Dealing with Writer's Block 65

Writing Resources 68

Where do I get ideas?... *69*

Writing software *71*

Should you join a professional writing association?.................................. *71*

National novel writing month (NaNoWriMo) young writers program
72

Writing partners.. *74*

First readers.. *75*

Choosing a Title.. 76

Dipping Your Feet in the Writing Pool Before Jumping In 80

Blogging *80*

Freelancing.. *82*

Contests *84*

Copyright and Legal Issues... 85

Editing and Revising.. 86

Revision tips... *86*

Chapter 3: Go... 91

How Traditional Publishing Works.. 91

What Happens After You Get a Publishing Deal?.............................. 94

Contract Basics 95

21st Century Publishing.. 97

The Big Five *98*

Other Publishing Options.. 100

Why self-publish?... *106*

CreateSpace *108*

Lulu *110*

A word of caution about vanity presses... *112*

Should You Hire a Freelance Editor? 114

Chapter 4: Publishing an E-book...117

Why E-Publish?..117

Identifying Your Audience..123

E-Publishing Options..125

Upload directly to an online retailer..............................125

Through an independent e-book distributor.................127

Sell directly from your website......................................129

E-Readers..130

Formatting..131

Creating content for e-readers...132

Protection from Copyright Infringement and Electronic Theft.....134

Digital Rights Management (DRM) software.................134

Pricing Your E-book..137

Chapter 5: Literary Agents..141

What Does a Literary Agent Do?...141

Do I Need a Literary Agent?...142

Am I Ready for an Agent?...144

How to Land a Literary Agent...146

Where Do I find a Literary Agent?......................................149

How to Decide if an Agent is Right for You.......................152

I Have an Agent, Now What?...157

Chapter 6: Putting Together Your Pitch Package.....................161

The Submission Process...161

The Pitch Package...162

The query letter *163*

Parts of a query letter *165*

Synopsis *167*

Proposals *169*

Chapter 7: Your Author Platform 177

Branding 178

Creating a Website 180

What should your website include? *181*

Where to get design ideas *182*

Social Networking 184

Podcasts *184*

The Big Two: Facebook and Twitter *185*

Online Chats *186*

Book trailers *187*

Creating your YouTube channel *188*

Book Signings, Readings, and Tours 189

Planning your event *189*

Unusual venues *196*

How to give a good reading even if you are terrified *198*

Author Pages 200

Goodreads author program *200*

Amazon author central *202*

Conclusion 205

Appendix A: Additional Resources 207

Books on Writing 207

Websites 209

Contests & Awards.. 209

Writing Conferences/Workshops/Classes 211

Professional Organizations 212

Glossary.. 213

Bibliography 217

Index... 225

About the Author 229

Foreword

Beth Reekles, young adult author

"Success" is a weird thing to think about. How does one become successful? What makes a writer successful? What does success even mean?

I'm a published author. I've been nominated for awards and spoken at several events. One of my novels, *The Kissing Booth*, has sold several translation rights and is set to be a Netflix original movie. But the time I really felt like a *successful* writer was the first time I believed in myself.

I've always liked writing—I think ever since I *could* write. When I was little, I thought it would be cool to be an author. That didn't change as I got older—I just realized how difficult it was to achieve. Yes, you had to write a book, a feat in itself, but then you couldn't just *get published*. You had to get an agent, who'd get you a publisher, and you'd probably face a slew of rejection letters along the way. After all, Harry Potter was rejected about a dozen times. It was difficult. Even more so when you don't believe in yourself.

I was always incredibly private about my writing. My family and friends had no idea I was devoting so much time to writing (my parents thought I was just on Facebook). I had no confidence in my ability or ideas, either.

Then I found Wattpad.

I say that like it was this big stage in my life, and it was. Wattpad is an on-line story-sharing platform where people can post and read stories for free. I began as a reader when I was 15, back in 2010, and it wasn't long before I was posting my own stories on the site.

On Wattpad, I could be as anonymous as I liked, and that appealed to me; I was so self-conscious about my writing, convinced it was terrible. But I thought, why not? If nobody read my story, I was no worse off. And if people liked it, they weren't just saying that because they were my friend and wanted to save my feelings; they *actually* liked it.

I began *The Kissing Booth* by initially posting three chapters—enough, I thought, for someone to decide if it was worth waiting a few days for the next part. At first, it was slow. I was refreshing my profile every ten min-utes, thrilled if there was one more read.

I uploaded regularly—at least once a week. (I wrote chapters in advance to make sure I always had something waiting to upload.) If I gained a fol-lower, I thanked him or her. I tried to respond to comments and messages, especially the ones asking questions. My fan base grew, and my readers were as dedicated to reading my story as I was to writing it.

The reads counter went from a few thousand, to hundreds of thousands, to millions. That was hard to wrap my head around—even more so for my parents, when I told them. (I did tell them eventually, of course—but still didn't let them read my work.) It was surreal to me that so many people were so invested in my book.

About halfway through posting *The Kissing Booth*, I remember uploading a chapter that ended with a horrendous cliff-hanger. I posted chapters in the evenings; a lot of my readers were from the U.S. and responded most to chapters uploaded in the afternoon in their time zone. So I uploaded my hideous cliff-hanger chapter, saw a few comments, and went to bed. The next morning I woke up to around three hundred emails—all comments on the latest chapter.

The response was phenomenal. Three hundred comments overnight? It was crazy.

That was when I first felt successful. That was the first time I took myself seriously. That kind of response made me step back and think, "Maybe I'm not so bad at this whole writing thing after all." People loved my story and were enthusiastic about my writing. And not just because they knew me and thought they owed me a nice response. They *really* loved it.

And that was a big deal for me.

I posted *The Kissing Booth* to Wattpad in 2011. By late 2012, it had over 19 million hits, and I was contacted by an editor at Penguin Random House and promptly offered a three-book deal. It's sold tens of thousands of copies worldwide, and at the time of writing this, it's in pre-production as a Netflix movie. Those are all phenomenal, crazy, surreal things, and nothing will ever match up to the feeling of being offered a book deal after pouring my heart and soul into a project.

But I didn't need any of those things to feel like a real, successful writer. I just needed to believe in myself.

The publishing industry has changed significantly in the last few years. Online and indie published authors aren't looked down on; they're taken seriously. Many of them go on to get traditional publishing deals, too. (And contrary to what some people believe, self-publishing your work online doesn't harm your chances of getting published. Without it, I wouldn't be where I am.)

So I encourage you to write. And more than that—to believe in yourself. Have faith in your ability, your ideas, your story. Share your work—whether it's with friends, or a supportive online community where you're totally anonymous. Build your confidence. Keep writing, keep creating. Your story matters. Your dreams and aspirations matter. It's up to you to make them a reality—and I wish you the best of luck.

Beth Reekles is a 21-year-old Young Adult author from South Wales and Physics graduate. She began posting her first novel, The Kissing Booth, *online to Wattpad when she was 15 years old, and when she was 17 she earned a three-book deal with Random House. In 2013, she was on the Time's Top 16 Most Influential Teens list, and in 2014 she was nominated for the Queen of Teen awards. Her current published works include:* The Kissing Booth, Rolling Dice, Out of Tune, *and* Cwtch Me If You Can.

Introduction

I can't remember a time when I wasn't writing. Although writing as a profession would come later (after different career paths), I was always scribbling a poem or other forms of creative expression since I learned how to hold a fat, stubby pencil.

Today, many young wordsmiths pursue writing careers at an early age. Why not? It's a great time to be a writer, and there are many opportunities to do so.

So you want to be a writer? You have picked up this guide, so I am going to assume you are vigorously shaking your head in the affirmative. Good. Many young writers before you have been bitten by the writing bug and went on to achieve great success.

After you publish your first book, you will join the ranks of young authors like:

- Amelia Atwater-Rhodes, a young adult urban fantasy writer who published her first book, *In the Forests of the Night*, in 1999, when she was 15
- Flavia Bujor who began writing her children's book, *The Prophecy of the Stones* (2002) when she was 12

- Juliette Davies who wrote the first book in the 4-book *JJ Halo* series when she was eight years old

- Mary Shelley who wrote *Frankenstein* when she was 19 and published it the following year

- Best-selling author Alec Greven who wrote his first book, *How to Talk to Girls,* when he was nine—he published four more books by the ripe old age of 11

Let's not forget the beautiful, although tragic account of Anne Frank's ordeal detailing the two years her family was in hiding during the Nazi occupation in the Netherlands, which was written when Anne was 13-15. *The Diary of Anne Frank* was published in 1947, after her death.

Are Two Heads Better Than One?
Young Twin Publishing Success Stories

Maybe it's something in their shared genetic code that makes twins ideal writing partners. Suresh and Jyoti Guptara wrote their first book at 11. *Conspiracy of Calaspia*, the first book in the *Insanity Saga*, was published when the twins were 17. Jyoti also has the distinction of having been both the world's youngest writer at the *Wall Street Journal*, and the world's youngest full-time writer at the age of 15.

Twins Brittany and Brianna Winner wrote their first book, *The Strand Prophecy*, at 12, and it became a national best seller by the time they turned 13. In addition to their four science fiction novels, they have published a writing book and several comic books. They are also dyslexic, but their disability didn't stop them from achieving success, all before their 18th birthday.

If you are ready to add your name to the list of published young writers, then this guide is definitely for you.

How to Use This Guide

The big question lingering on the tip of your tongue may be: how can this guide help me become a published author? This is an excellent question, and fortunately I have the perfect answer. This authoritative book will guide you step-by-step as you navigate the road to seeing your dreams of authorship become a reality.

Becoming a successful writer—at any age—is no longer a pipe dream. This book will show you how. Before you start writing your manuscript, it is important to take some time to evaluate if you have what it takes to succeed in the world of publishing.

I am not talking about having the skill set to write; I believe that anyone who truly desires to become a writer can learn writing techniques. That is why we have creative writing classes. Before you start writing, there are many considerations you should explore. We will do just that in the first chapter.

This book will cover important topics to ponder, like how to handle rejection. Rejection is an inevitable part of the writing life. It's not a matter of "if" it will happen but "when." This guide will help you learn to bounce back from the inevitable so that you can keep writing. This book will also cover topics such as sticking to a regular writing routine, handling success *and* criticism, an overview of publishing options, and more.

If you haven't already decided on your genre, don't worry. In Chapter 2, we take a look at popular genres. You'll see explanations of each along with examples. Then, we move on to information that will help you sharpen your writing skills. Should you take an online class? Is a writing group for you?

Chapter 2 also covers information on where to get ideas, how to deal with writer's block, how to choose a title, and more. It will also cover ways you can get writing experience while you work on your manuscript. Plus, we'll offer some editing and revising tips.

Moving on to Chapter 3, you will learn more about the publishing process. Your manuscript is written and polished to a shine, so now it's time to start sending it out to agents and publishers. But before that, you need to understand the basics of the publishing process, who the major players are, and what your publishing options are. Chapter 3 has you covered.

Some people have been saying for years that print is dead, but a printed book is not your only option. Many authors choose e-book publishing in lieu of or in addition to a print option for their books. Chapter 4 will discuss everything you need to know about electronic publishing including why you might consider this option, formatting your book, and the different types of e-book devices.

Do you need a literary agent? Most of the major publishing houses require authors to submit their work through a literary agent. Chapter 5 will help you understand the role of literary agents and where to find one.

But before you send your manuscript off to an agent or directly to a publisher, you will learn how to best present your work in a professional manner. This includes learning the basics of writing a book proposal and query. Chapter 6 will cover this topic along with additional useful information such as an overview of the submissions process and how to put together the perfect pitch package.

You may think that once your manuscript is written and you have landed a publishing contract that all the hard work is over. In some ways, the hard work has just begun. Relax, this book will continue to guide you, even after you have a signed contract.

You will need to build your writer's platform. Your platform will establish who you are as a writer and entice readers to buy your book. Very few people will learn how awesome your book is if you don't take time to create a buzz. Chapter 7 will equip you with information you can use to create your writer's platform including creating a website, blog, or YouTube channel.

This chapter will also discuss using social networking, book signings, tours, and more.

To equip you with resources you need to succeed as a writer, the appendix lists useful books, websites, contests, awards, and more.

It is definitely a great time to be a writer. If you are ready to begin your journey, turn the page, and let's get started.

Chapter 1: *Get Ready*

You have made the decision to move forward and publish your work of art. Congratulations! Before you put pen to paper—or start tapping away on your keyboard—there are a few things you should think about first.

Writing is hard work. Forget about the people who romanticize the writing life. You know the ones I'm talking about. They brag about pounding out bestsellers while sitting on the beach, sipping refreshing mocktails or guzzling down iced chai lattes. Agents, editors, and publishers adore them, they claim. Six-figure deals are thrown at these authors like hot potatoes.

In the real world, this probably will not happen to you. Don't get me wrong—you can have a successful writing career, but you need to prepare yourself for the downside of the writing life. Writing a book for fun or profit is certainly an achievable goal if you are willing to put in the work.

Considerations on the Writing Life

Let's take a short quiz. Before you start your writing journey, there are a few key questions to consider. Don't worry—you don't have to share your answers with anyone.

Unless you want to.

Here we go.

Can you handle rejection?

When I first started my freelance writing career many years ago, I was fortunate. I sold ideas to the first three publications I approached. Then something unheard of (at least to me) happened; I received my first rejection.

To say that I was devastated would be an understatement. How dare they reject me! It doesn't matter if you plan to publish only one book or make a career from your writing, rejection is something you will have to deal with. It's a fact of life. Let me highlight this important statement for you:

Every writer, at some point in his or her career will get rejected.

When you send your manuscript off, one day you will receive the inevitable— a standard rejection letter.

```
Dear Hopeful Writer,

Thank you for giving me the opportunity to
read your manuscript. Unfortunately, your
story is not a good fit for us at this
time. Good luck with your writing.

Sincerely,

Ed I. Tor

Ed I. Tor
XYZ Book Publisher
```

When rejection comes, consider yourself in good company. There is a long and growing list of writers who received rejection letters but went on to achieve literary excellence, including Stephen King, J.K. Rowling, J.D. Salinger, Stephanie Meyer, William Golding, C.S. Lewis, and L. Frank Baum. Even our beloved Dr. Seuss knew a thing or two about rejection.[1]

Like death and taxes, you cannot escape the dreaded rejection letter (or email). Just remember you should not mistake rejection of your idea with rejection of you as a person. You have to—as Taylor Swift said—shake it off. What you choose to do with your rejection letters is up to you. You can:

- Stuff them in a file folder

- Use them to wallpaper your room

- Set fire to them (Just kidding, setting fire to stuff is not cool.)

Whatever you decide, don't let a rejection stop you from sending your manuscript to other agents or publishers. If you keep trying, eventually you can find a home for your work.

Do not expect to get much of an explanation as to why your manuscript was rejected. With thousands of manuscripts landing on the desks and inboxes of editors and publishers, it's impossible to respond to each hopeful with a personalized message. Sure, it would be great if you received feedback. It would help you figure out what you did wrong. More likely, you will receive a standard rejection form letter. Or worse—you may not receive a response at all. Again, it's nothing personal.

If you *are* one of lucky few, you may receive a personalized message or a short note scribbled at the bottom of the form letter. I once received a

---

1. **www.litrejections.com**, 2016.

standard rejection letter from a magazine I was trying to break into. There was a short, sticky note of praise attached. I submitted a different idea, and the editor accepted it. That short note told me exactly what the editor needed. She liked my writing but was over-saturated with similar ideas. Having an idea of what she was looking for gave me a leg up on the pool of other freelancers hungry for assignments.

If you receive a personal message, take it as a sign of encouragement. Read the message carefully, and then act on it. If the message offered suggestions on ways to improve the marketability of your manuscript, follow through.

Why your manuscript may get rejected

Your book idea may be rejected for many reasons, but here are three of the most popular ones.

It doesn't fit with the goals of the publishing company. It's important to read the publisher's guidelines. If a publisher doesn't publish poetry, no matter how wonderful you think your manuscript is, you will receive a rejection letter. Similarly, if a publisher of children's books clearly says they don't want to read manuscripts with talking animals or books that rhyme, then don't send manuscripts that go against the guidelines. You may think your work is so great that they will make an exception for you, but they won't.

A sluggish economy may mean publishers are accepting fewer books. One of the reasons some writers turn to self-publishing is because they realize that when the economy is ugly, publishers will hand out fewer contracts. Publishing is a business, and the goal is to make money.

If a publisher is handing out fewer contracts, who do you think will get one?

A) An unknown, first time author without a following

B) An established, multi-published author with a gazillion readers in his or her fan base

If you answered "B," move to the front of the class. Before you jump over James Patterson, Stephen King, or J.K. Rowling and snag a deal during tough times, you'd better have one heck of an irresistible manuscript — one that a publisher would be foolish to pass up. If you have access to a famous person, for instance, you can probably land a deal without any problems.

The publisher may have already accepted a similar book. Have you ever read a book and thought, "This reminds me of . . . ?" Although you may think your idea is 100 percent original, you can probably count on someone else having a similar thought. If someone beat you to the punch, the publisher will not risk publishing two similar books.

Can you handle success?

I know this question may seem odd. But, you need to be prepared to handle the success that may come with publishing a book. Most writers dream of publishing a successful book. They imagine reaching the top of best sellers' lists, of jetting around the world making appearances on all of the popular talk shows.

Sometimes, there's a price for success. Can you handle it? Throughout the history of publishing, many authors have not been able to. A lot of writers are introverted. We like to be alone with our thoughts. Being thrust into the spotlight can cause stress or anxiety. Well-known author J.D. Salinger (*Catcher in the Rye*), for example, was equally as famous for living a reclusive life as he was for being a great writer.

Can you take constructive criticism?

You may hover over your writing, protecting it like a mama bear protects her cubs, but eventually someone's going to have to actually read your creation. Not wanting to hurt your feelings, friends and loved ones may have nothing but loud praise for your work. But just like rejection, you can expect some criticism of your work. You can't get "all up in your feelings" and overreact when someone criticizes your work.

Whether it's an editor, a writing group, a family member, etc., take the critique and learn from it.

In addition to constructive criticism, can you handle criticism in general? Some writers devote a lot of time worrying about book critics. When your book is published, critics will review it. You can expect some negative reviews. People may go on Amazon.com and trash your work. Some of these fakers may not have even read your book. Some writers will brush critics off like flaky dandruff on a new black suit. Others will not be able to move on from negative reviews. They may start to doubt their ability as a writer. Some writers are so traumatized they may never publish again.

Do you have the skills to write—or can you learn?

When people find out that I'm a writer, they often lament on their own desire to write. I get this question a lot: "How can I become a writer, like you?" Well, duh, there's no big secret to writing. I always tell inquiring minds that the secret to becoming a writer is to . . . wait for it . . . actually write.

You will never become a writer if you sit around thinking about becoming a writer. Just like sitting in a garage all day and night will not, through osmosis, turn you into a car. There is a process to writing a book. As Walter Dean Myers penned in *Just Write: Here's How!,*

"A book doesn't just appear out of nowhere."[2]

There is no such thing as a book fairy. You will not drift off to sleep staring at an empty page, only to wake up and find a perfectly written, perfectly formatted manuscript. If you want to write a book, you need the skills necessary to make that happen. Or you need a way to acquire these skills.

CASE STUDY: ANNA CALTABIANO

As a teenager or a young adult, it's easy to have doubts about the value of one's writing. What do I have to offer that hasn't been written better by someone older and more successful than I? Why should I be writing this story and not someone else? But the answer to that is simple. You're writing this story because you're you; you're approaching this story with your own background—youth and all. You are writing about your life as you grow and have important unique experiences that shape your life. Having a crush on the guy from Algebra, failing that midterm—countless seemingly inconsequential experiences define who you are and what you could become. Only you can write this story.

Anna Caltabiano is an up-and-coming young adult author who has already published three widely acclaimed novels—the first when she was only 15. She was born in British colonial Hong Kong and educated in Mandarin Chinese schools before moving to Palo Alto, California.

---

2. Myers, 2012.

Can you stick to a writing routine?

Sticking to a regular writing schedule is probably the hardest thing for many writers (and wanna be writers) to do. As I said earlier, writing is hard. Sometimes when you sit down to write, the words will flow like sweet syrup down a stack of buttery pancakes. At other times, not so much.

Gail Carson Levine writes in *Writer to Writer: From Think to Ink,* that writing ". . . isn't always pleasurable, even for people who love to write."[3] I love to write. But sometimes I love to sleep. I love to sit in my backyard, drinking coffee (and wonder why my neighbor's cat is lounging at my feet).

But, you have to be able to push through any problems you encounter during your designated writing time. You can't get distracted by shiny objects, get frustrated when the ideas are stagnant, or mad because your muse Calliope has left you hanging once again.

There's no universal writer routine handbook you can flip through to find a schedule that works for you. Writers have different routines, and you will have to find your own flow. Some authors like to write for a certain amount of time, while others will write until they reach a particular word count or number of pages. You may feel more creative and productive early in the mornings. For others, writing in the middle of the day or late at night is what gets their imaginative juices flowing.

Some writing resource books recommend scheduling time to write like it was any other important appointment. That's right—schedule time for writing. Actually put it on your calendar. Most importantly, keep the appointment.

---

3. Levine, 1993.

Can you meet deadlines?

When you're hammering out the first draft of your book, you may not have a deadline to meet (unless you're under contract); it's easy to kick back and write at your leisure. There will come a time when you will have to meet a deadline. Will you be able to do it?

Let's look at a scenario:

Your manuscript has been bought by a publisher. Yeah, yours! The editor has gone through your manuscript and made editorial changes. She has returned the manuscript with comments. She expects you to go through the comments and make the changes she needs. She gives you a deadline for returning the manuscript with the incorporated changes. Can you do it?

You do not want to stop the flow of the publishing process by not meeting deadlines. Sometimes, you may have to make sacrifices.

It's Thursday. You're under a tight deadline. You have to return your manuscript on Monday. But you planned to go to the movies with your BFF on Friday. You had a date night scheduled with your boo on Saturday. Sunday? Well, you planned on sleeping in late.

With deadlines looming, sacrifices will have to be made. As a freelancer, I have had to work on assignments during holidays, on weekends, during family emergencies, on my birthday, when I was under the weather, etc. in order to make a deadline. That's all part of the writing life.

Editors aren't monsters and will usually work with you if a problem comes up, as long as you give sufficient notice. Contacting an editor two hours before a deadline to ask for an extension is a big no-no. Even when you don't have a deadline, it's still a good idea to set a self-imposed one so that you get in the habit of finishing work in a set time frame.

Can you keep writing in the face of adversity?

You have decided that you want to publish a book. You have established a writing routine. You regularly schedule appointments with yourself to write. You are confident that you can deal with criticism and rejection. Everything is moving smoothly.

Until:

Your car breaks down.
You wake up with a killer headache.
There's four feet of snow outside.
Your friends are going out for pizza and a movie.

There will be times when you have to keep writing—no matter what is going on around you. If not, you will never complete your manuscript.

Do you need a dedicated workspace?

I have a dedicated home office. Most of the time, I write in this space. But, I also write at a desk in my bedroom, on my sofa in the living room, in my bed, and in the backyard. I write at the library. I have written in my car, while sitting in the parking lot waiting for my son to be dismissed from school or finish an after-school event. I have written during my morning walk around the park and while standing in line at the grocery store. And yes, I write (not often though) from a coffee shop. There is a point to my rambling—you can literally write from anywhere.

My question is, "Do you need a dedicated "writing" space?" The author Virginia Woolf famously wrote that a woman should have ". . . a room of her own if she is to write fiction."[4]

I will piggyback on that statement. I think it is important for all serious writers to have a writing space in their home. It's perfectly fine to write at other venues, but I think having a space you can call your own sets the tone for your writing sessions. When you sit down to write "in your space," a message is sent to your brain that it's time to get down to business.

---

4. Woolf, 1929.

In *Writing Down the Bones,* author Natalie Goldberg suggests writing under different circumstances and in different places. Let's face it—unless you're a hermit living alone far removed from civilization, there are times when you will have to write, tuning out the noise buzzing around your head. Goldberg suggests writing in various locations including trains, the bus, the curb in front of your house, the back seat of a car, or in the waiting room at the dentist's office. Basically, write from wherever you are and from wherever you feel comfortable.

This concludes the test portion of Chapter 1. How did you do? If you answered each question with an enthusiastic (or semi-enthusiastic) "Yes!" then it's time to move ahead and make your publishing dreams a reality. Next step? Deciding which route to publishing you will take.

How Will You Publish?

Once you decide to publish, you have an important decision to make. Will you approach a traditional publisher, or will you self-publish? Chapter 3 will discuss publishing options in more detail, but it's a good idea to decide which route you want to take before you actually begin writing your manuscript.

You can always change your mind later, but having a plan in motion will help you focus. For example, if you know you will definitely self-publish, you won't have to spend time looking for a literary agent. Please don't skip over Chapter 5 of this guide, though. It's a good idea to learn about literary agents for future work. Also, it's possible your self-published book will do so well that an agent will come looking for you! It's never a bad idea to have a working knowledge of how agents operate.

If you don't plan to self-publish, then you'll have to decide which option is right for you. Will you try for one of the large publishing houses or a small press?

Once you decide which publishing avenue you plan to take, it's time to get down to writing.

Are you ready? In their book, *The Essential Guide to Getting Your Book Published*, Arielle Eckstut and David Henry Sterry, write that the real question is: ". . . do you have the skill, audacity, brains, drive, the *vavavoom* and *zazazoo* to write a book, find someone to publish it and then convince people to buy it?"[5]

This perfectly sums up what you need to consider before beginning your writing project.

If you are ready to move on, we will dive into the mechanics of writing your book.

---

5. Eckstut and Sterry, 2010.

Chapter 2: *Get Set*

Before you begin writing your book, you will need to choose a genre. Genre refers to a "kind, category, or sort, esp of literary or artistic work," according to dictionary.com.[6] It is essential that you know which genre your book falls into before approaching a publisher. Why?

Glad you asked. The easiest way to get rejected by a publisher is to send them a manuscript in a genre they do not normally publish. No matter how great and wonderful you feel your Young Adult manuscript is, if the publisher only publishes romance books, you will not get a publishing deal.

When you start looking for a publisher, you will need to do your homework (yes, writing involves *a lot* of homework) to make sure you approach publishers that specialize in your chosen genre. Genres are also useful because they help bookstores and libraries categorize books, making it easy for readers to quickly locate reading material. Within some genre categories, you will find sub-genres. A sub-genre is a book category that is ". . . a subdivision of a larger genre."[7]

---

6. Dictionary.com, 2016.
7. Dictionary.com, 2016.

Choosing Your Genre

You have many genres at your disposal. I will not list them all, because I know that you are anxious to get started with your writing. Plus, it's *wayyyyyy* too many to list. To get started, let's take a look at some of the more popular fiction and non-fiction genres.

Fiction

Romance

According to the Romance Writers of America, "Two basic elements comprise every romance novel: a central love story and an emotionally satisfying and optimistic ending."[8]

---

8. rwa.org, 2016.

Most romance novels follow a *boy-meets-girl-then-falls-madly-in-love* kind of scenario. You can expect conflict along the way before the plot reaches its conclusion.

Examples: *A Walk to Remember* by Nicholas Sparks; *Twilight* by Stephenie Meyer; and *The Fault in Our Stars* by John Green.

Sub-genres include: contemporary (1950 to the present time), historical (before 1950), inspirational, paranormal, suspense, and young adult.

Horror

Fear of the unknown. To me, this simple definition sums up the horror genre. The Horror Writers Association points out that a horror novel does not have to ". . . be full of ghosts, ghouls, and things to go bump in the night."[9] It is the emotional reaction readers experience—feelings of fear or dread—that is the hallmark of a good work of horror.

Examples: *End of Watch* by Stephen King (or anything by King!); *The Silence of the Lambs* by Thomas Harris; and *Frankenstein* by Mary Shelley.

Sub-genres include: comic horror, creepy kids, dark fantasy, gothic, hauntings, psychological, supernatural menace, technology, weird tales, young adult, and zombie.

Thriller/Suspense

The Writer's Encyclopedia defines thriller as a work intended to ". . . arouse feelings of excitement or suspense."[10] Plots may involve illegal activities, espionage, and violence.

---

9. **www.horror.org,** 2009.
10. Writer's Digest, 1996.

According to Goodreads, "Thrillers are characterized by fast pacing, frequent action, and resourceful heroes who must thwart the plans of more-powerful and better-equipped villains."[11]

Suspense novels are often clumped together with thrillers. With suspense novels, readers are unsure about the outcome. This leads to ". . . a feeling of uncertainty and anxiety . . ." (on the part of the reader).[12]

Examples: *The Girl on the Train* by Paula Hawkins; *The Whistler* by John Grisham; and *Sharp Objects* by Gillian Flynn.

Sub-genres include: action, conspiracy, crime, espionage, legal, medical, military, police, political, psychological, romantic, supernatural, and technological.

Science Fiction

Science fiction novels—or sci-fi as it is affectionately called—center around how science and technology impact society. The setting often takes place in a world very different from our own, with many of the novels taking place in the future.

Science fiction novels are rooted in scientific fact but writers, of course, take certain liberties. In *The Writer's Encyclopedia*, it is noted that the science is ". . . hypothesized from known facts . . ."[13]

Examples: *The Hunger Games* by Suzanne Collins; *I am Legend* by Richard Matheson; and *The Maze Runner* by James Dashner.

---

11. **www.goodreads.com,** 2016.
12. **www.goodreads.com,** 2016.
13. Writer's Digest, 1996.

Subgenres include: dystopian, mystical, post-apocalyptic, space opera, steampunk, superheroes, thriller, time-travel, and young adult.

Fantasy

A cousin to sci-fi is the fantasy novel. According to *The Writer's Encyclopedia*, there is often a thin line between the two genres. However, to be classified as fantasy, the novel relies on ". . . magic, mythological and neo-mythological beings and devices, and outright inventions for conflict and setting."[14]

Examples: *Fantastic Beasts and Where to Find Them* by J.K. Rowling; *Miss Peregrine's Home for Peculiar Children* by Ransom Riggs; and *Wicked Lovely* by Marissa Marr.

Sub-genres include: cyber punk, dystopian, heroic, mythic, new age, romance, science fantasy, steampunk, superheroes, sword and sorcery, time-travel, urban, vampire, and young adult.

Mystery/Crime

In a mystery novel, a crime is in need of solving. Plain and simple. The star of the novel may be a seasoned detective(s) or an amateur sleuth. The crime often involves a mysterious death. However, the plot could involve any type of crime. This type of novel is sprinkled with actual clues or purposefully misleading clues — red herrings. The reader follows along (and tries to solve the mystery) until the big reveal at the end of the novel.

Examples: *Gone Girl* by Gillian Flynn; *The Girl Who Played with Fire* by Stieg Larsson; and *The DaVinci* Code by Dan Brown.

---

14. Writer's Digest, 1996.

Sub-genres include: amateur detective, classic whodunit, comic (bungling detective), cozy, courtroom, espionage, forensic, heists and capers, historical, police procedural, private detective, psychological, romantic, suspense, and young adult.

Action-Adventure

The focus of this type of novel is on fast-paced action, rather than on character development. There is a sense of danger involved and the setting may take place in exotic locations.

Examples: *The Hunt for Red October* by Tom Clancy; *Mayan Secrets* by Clive Cussler; and *Ender's Game* by Orson Scott Card.

Sub-genres include: disaster, espionage, industrial/financial, medical, political intrigue, military and naval, survival, thriller, and western.

Historical

Historical fiction takes place in the past and uses characters or events from that time period. According to Goodreads, "Historical fiction may include fictional characters, well-known historical figures or a mixture of the two."[15]

Examples: *The Underground Railroad* by Colson Whitehead; *The Book Thief* by Markus Zusak; and *The Help* by Kathryn Stockett.

Sub-genres include: alternate histories, historical fantasies, and multiple-time novels.

---

15. **www.goodreads.com.**

Young Adult

The book you are reading falls within the young adult (YA) genre—although it is in the non-fiction category. Young Adult books are written for 12 to 18 year-olds (roughly). The protagonist or hero of the story is a young adult, and the plot revolves around his or her point of view. Young Adult novels are found in all genres of fiction. Typical plots include issues and challenges of the being a teen and coming of age stories.

Examples: *The Giver* by Lois Lowry; *The Perks of Being a Wallflower* by Stephen Chbosky; and *Holes* by Louis Sachar.

Sub-genres include: adventure, chick lit, diaries, contemporary fiction, dystopian, fantasy, horror, and graphic novels.

New Adult

This is a relatively new genre of fiction. New adult fiction, according to Goodreads, serves as a bridge between young adult and adult fiction. The hero of the novel is typically between the ages of 18 and 30. The plot centers around issues of concern to those in this age group, including leaving home for college or starting a full-time job.

According to Goodreads, this genre is a ". . . a subcategory of adult literature rather than young adult literature."[16] All genres of adult fiction are represented including romance, horror, sci-fi, etc. The subject matter covers more adult themes that are typically not found in Young Adult books. Examples include *Losing It*, by Cora Carmack, and *Walking Disaster*, by Jamie McGuire.

---

16. **www.goodreads.com.**

Genre vs Literary Fiction

Another aspect of writing fiction is deciding if you want to write literary or genre fiction. You need to know the distinction, because some publishers will only accept one or the other. So what's the difference?

Genre fiction refers to mass-produced tales, with a strong emphasis on plot. Genre fiction is also sometimes called popular fiction, and it appeals to a large audience.

On the other hand, for writers of literary fiction, "... style and technique are often as important as subject matter."[17] Mass-market appeal is also not an important factor for literary writers.

If you think about the types of fiction you read in English class, the majority of these novels fall within the literary fiction genre. *The Great Gatsby*, by F. Scott Fitzgerald, is an example of literary fiction.

CASE STUDY: NARESH VISSA

#1 Best Selling Author

The first element of a successful book is writing on a particular subject with a clear focus and expertise. The narrower the topic, the better.

The book you're currently reading, for example, is all about book publishing ... how to ideate, write, publish, and market a book completely on your own, step by step.

---

17. Writer's Encyclopedia, 1996.

That's a niche. You know, as a reader, what to expect when you read the title or buy the book.

As a writer, you must have the knowledge to discuss a topic in depth. It should be something that you are passionate about or are screaming to say. It's tough to pretend to feel an emotion or passion if you don't feel it.

You should write a book on a focused, narrow topic that you care about and want an audience to learn about. Many times, I write because I know I have strong, convincing arguments and points on certain subjects, but my friends and family won't listen to me because they aren't interested or are too busy with their lives. They don't want to hear me ramble about book publishing or digital marketing. So, my solution is to write a book for myself. The people who are interested will come later. If the book is good, then they will find your stuff.

Don't waste your time trying to become a hack author — someone who writes about random topics just because they're trending on Amazon, Google Trends, or Twitter. It's impossible to be an expert in disconnected subject areas, and if you're just writing because you think you'll sell many copies, then you'll quickly be labeled as a hack whose writing isn't genuine.

Businesses *must* take into account every trend and disruption because people start businesses with the intent of ultimately generating profits. An entrepreneur can't afford to ignore trends.

But book writing isn't the exact same as starting a business. This is because writing must be deep and unique in order to make an impact on the readers who are smart enough to purchase and take the time to read your book. They'll be smart enough to identify the author as a phony, too.

The best books — the ones that last through history — are the ones that were written out of sheer enthusiasm and choice. They're not the ones based off a Google Trend to make a quick buck.

But in your enthusiasm, be careful not to be too personal. People who tell me they want to write books say they want to share their "life story." I've written several books, and none have been about my life story. I could've written my life story if I wanted to, but I'm not really sure what my life story is. It could be about studying, working, failures, successes, friendships, relationships, girls, basketball, my family, or one of a hundred other topics.

Most people don't know their life stories. They're a bunch of disconnected events and experiences. Jumbled ideas don't make for good books.

I *have* shared some stories *from my life* in my books . . . but none of the books have been about my "life story."

Since your friends won't break it to you, I will: Unless you're a public figure, nobody cares about your "life story." Very few no-name authors become bestselling celebrities because of the autobiographies they write. They were likely famous first, so they had a platform to sell their books to.

Stephen Covey and Eckart Tolle didn't write their life stories . . . neither did Darwin, Machiavelli, or Freud. They instead took instances from their life to tell stories greater than themselves.

Maya Angelou, Malcolm X and Stephen King wrote their life stories in autobiographies. The books are classics. They are critically acclaimed.

But you're not Maya Angelou, Malcolm X, or Stephen King. Once you get to their level, you can publish your life story.

Until then, focus on what you're good at. That's where you need to start.

*Naresh Vissa (**www.nareshvissa.com**) is founder and CEO of Krish Media & Marketing (**www.krishmediamarketing.com**) and author of the #1 best-selling books* Fifty Shades of Market: Whip Your Business Into Shape and Dominate Your Competition *and* Podcastnomics: The Book of Podcasting . . . To Make You Millions.

Nonfiction

This wonderful guide you are reading is a nonfiction book. Merriam-Webster offers a simple definition of nonfiction: "writing that is about facts or real events."[18]

The goal of a nonfiction book is to help the reader. Nonfiction writers help readers by:

---

18. Merriam-webster.com, 2016.

- **Fixing a problem:** Self-help, how-to, reference, inspirational, travel guides, and cookbooks fall in this category.

- **Providing information to expand a reader's knowledge and world-view:** Types of work that fall in this category include memoirs, biographies, autobiographies, historical accounts, and books on current events.

You may think that your age disqualifies you from nonfiction writing. But that's not the case. Successful nonfiction writers are good at researching and then translating the information so that it is easily understood by the average reader. If you are good at researching, consider writing a nonfiction book. Let's take a closer look at a few of the most popular types of nonfiction books, and then you can decide for yourself.

How-to

The awesome book you are reading (I know, I know, I'm repeating myself and tooting my own horn!) is an example of a how-to book. When you finish this guide, you will be armed with the knowledge you need to successfully publish a book or e-book. My work will be done, and it will be up to you whether you succeed or not. I have confidence that you will, though.

Where was I? Oh, right, how-to books. How-to books are extremely popular and generally sell well. Types of how-to books include: business, career, money, dieting, and health/fitness.

How-to books are filled with instructions, valuable tips, suggestions, and examples. The information is presented in an orderly sequential format. Each chapter supports the overall vision of the book. If readers follow the plan presented in the book, they should achieve their goal.

Examples: *The Young Adult's Guide to Robert's Rules of Order: How to Run Meetings for Your Club or Organization* by Hannah Litwiller; *On Writing*, by Stephen King; *Adulting: How to Become a Grown-up in 468 Easy(ish) Steps* by Kelly Williams Brown; and *How to Travel the World on $50 a Day: Travel Cheaper, Longer, Smarter* by Matt Kepnes.

Self-Help

If you have recently broken up with your boo, you may turn to a self-help book to get you through the tough times. Self-help books are written to instruct readers on how to handle personal problems, like relationships.

This is a popular category. A quick check on Amazon returned **853,934** self-help books. And counting. The numbers will certainly rise by the time this book is printed. The books are often written by experts in their field (or self-proclaimed experts), although anyone can write a self-help book. This is particularly true if the author has first-hand experience on the subject matter.

Examples: *The Young Adult's Long-Distance Relationship Survival Guide: Tips, Tricks & Expert Advice for Being Apart and Staying Happy* by Atlantic Publishing; *#GIRLBOSS* by Sophia Amoruso; *I'm Judging You: The Do-Better Manual* by Luvvie Ajayi; and *Show Your Work!: 10 Ways to Share Your Creativity and Get Discovered* by Austin Kleon.

Travel Guides

You may have picked up a copy of *Fodor's* or *Frommer's* travel guide before a vacation or if you're like me, to daydream about someday visiting some exotic locale. Travel guides, especially ones written by locals, are in high demand. Guides with unique spins or that target a certain demographic are also highly desired. For example, guides for parents traveling with young kids, for older adult travelers, or for single travelers are all good choices. A teen's travel guide written by a teen is also a good choice, so feel free to add that to your list of possible book ideas.

Examples: *A Walk in the Woods: Rediscovering America on the Appalachian Trail* by Bill Bryson; *Vagabonding: An Uncommon Guide to the Art of Long-Term World Travel* by Rolf Potts; and *1,000 Places to See Before You Die* by Patricia Schultz.

Cooking and Food

Besides eating, one of my favorite activities is browsing through cookbooks. I am fortunate to live within walking distance of one of the branches of my local library, and I will spend an hour or so hanging out in the cookbook section.

If you have a knack for creating delicious dishes, you may want to consider putting together your own cookbook. Or you can publish a family cookbook. Like travel guides written by teens, a teen cookbook is an idea a publisher may be very open to. A cookbook could also be a quick entrance into the publishing world.

With so many cookbooks on the market, you need a distinctive theme that will make a reader pick up—or view online—then ultimately buy your book. For me, my pet peeve is cookbooks without pictures. I need a picture of *every. single. recipe.* I need to see what the finished product is supposed to look like. I also don't like recipes with too many ingredients. If I have to scrounge up more than a dozen ingredients, count me out. So I am personally drawn to cookbooks that fit within those parameters.

Examples: *101 Recipes for Making Cheese: Everything You Need to Know Explained Simply* by Cynthia Martin; *Feeding Hannibal: A Connoisseur's Cookbook* by Janice Poon (recipes inspired by the hit TV show); *Yes, Chef* by Marcus Samuelsson; and *The Bob's Burgers Burger Book: Real Recipes for Joke Burgers* by Loren Bouchard.

Humor

If you have the gift of making others laugh, a humor book may be in your future. Personally, I think I am at my funniest when I'm not trying to be funny, so I'm not sure I could write an entire book filled with tidbits of my witty repartee.

Examples: *Scrappy Little Nobody* by Anna Kendrick; *Talking as Fast as I Can: From Gilmore Girls to Gilmore Girls, and Everything in Between* by Lauren Graham; and *You Can't Touch My Hair: And Other Things I Still Have to Explain* by Phoebe Robinson.

Creative Nonfiction

Also known as narrative nonfiction, this genre combines elements of a novel—like plot, conflict, and dialogue—to tell a real-life story. In other words, the words flows like a work of fiction, but it is, in fact, nonfiction. Popular subgenres include:

Adventure

Adventure tales pit man against nature, often in exotic locations facing extreme danger.

Examples: *Into Thin Air: A Personal Account of the Mount Everest Disaster* by Jon Krakauer; *Touching the Void: The True Story of One Man's Miraculous Survival* by Joe Simpson; and *Adrift: Seventy-Six Days Lost at Sea* by Steven Callahan.

Travelogues

A travelogue is a detailed accounting of an author's travel experience. These books may include travel guide details about the destination.

Examples: *Travelogue from an Unruly Youth* by D. C. Jesse Burkhardt; *The Wander Year: One Couple's Journey Around the World* by Mike McIntyre; and *1000 Days of Spring: Travelogue of a Hitchhiker* by Tomislav Perko.

Biography

A biography is a detailed account of a person's life. The subject can be living or dead, famous or infamous. Typically, biographies start at the beginning—the subject's birth—and proceed chronologically. Biographies may also start at a significant point in the subjects' life. Either way, the biographies usually progress in time, ending with the subjects' death, another significant point in time, or in the present day. For example, one biography of President Obama, written years after the end of his terms, could detail his years in the White House and end with his last days in office. Another one could start at birth and end with his first inauguration. A third book could highlight a specific incident in his life.

The key to a good biography is to do your homework (I told you there would be homework, so stop grumbling). If you decide to write a biography, here are some important questions to ask yourself:

- Can you count on the cooperation of the subject (if alive) or family members to assist in telling his or her story?

- How will fans react to negative disclosures?

- Is the market already overly saturated on the subject? If so, can you offer new information, insights or perspectives not previously covered?

- Will you provide cradle-to-grave coverage, or chose an important event or portion of your subject's life to focus on?

Examples: *People That Changed the Course of History: The Story of Frank Lloyd Wright 150 Years After His Birth* by Hannah Sandoval; *Alexander Hamilton* by Ron Chernow; *Einstein: His Life and Universe* by Walter Isaacson; and *Born to Run Hardcover* by Bruce Springsteen.

Memoir

I remember an old commercial for the Navy that asked: "If someone wrote a book about your life, would anyone want to read it?" My life so far has been pretty boring, but maybe you have a story to tell that may inspire, entertain, or uplift readers.

A memoir is a personal account of your life—tragic or inspiring. Your story should also have universal appeal so that you can connect with readers.

Examples: *My Life as an OB-GYN: A Look Behind the Scenes* by Douglas Heritage; *North of Normal: A Memoir of My Wilderness Childhood, My Unusual Family, and How I Survived* by Cea Sunrise Person; *The Year We Disappeared: A Father - Daughter Memoir* by Cylin Busby; and *Long Journey Home: A Young Girl's Memoir of Surviving the Holocaust* by Lucy Lipiner.

True Crime

True crime stories are ones "ripped from the headlines" that explore real-life crimes. Successful true crime writers are adept at investigating, have superior analytical skills, and are knowledgeable about police and forensic procedures. These stories generally offer an in-depth study of relevant characters, including the victim, the victim's family, the detectives, the lawyers, and the perpetrator (if known).

Examples: *The BASEMENT: True Crime Serial Killer Gary Heidnik* by RJ Parker Ph.D.; *Who Killed These Girls?: Cold Case: The Yogurt Shop Murders* by Beverly Lowry; and *True Crime: Deadly Serial Killers and Gruesome Murders Stories from the Last 100 Years* by Hank Gatsby.

Essays

You no doubt are familiar with essay writing. You have probably written a few during your school career. You may have an essay due in English Composition even as we speak. Perhaps you are sick and tired of writing essays.

Or maybe your essays leave tears in the eyes of all who read them. If so, you may want to consider putting together a book of essays as your first writing project.

With an essay, a writer takes a subject and expands on it. The writer is generally arguing for or against a subject.

Examples: *The Opposite of Loneliness: Essays and Stories* by Marina Keegan; *Slouching Towards Bethlehem: Essays* by Joan Didion; and *Consider the Lobster and Other Essays* by David Foster Wallace.

As you can see, there are many genres ripe for the picking. While some authors write in only one genre, many publish in multiple genres. You don't have to pick only one. That's the beauty of being a writer. We have so many choices.

Sharpening Your Writing Skills

Although writing may come naturally for you, it's still a good idea to sharpen your writing skills. There are many ways you can learn to write better. Let's go over a few suggestions.

Writing Classes & Workshops

If you are looking to sharpen your writing chops, you may want to consider taking a writing class or workshop. You can find classes in your community or take an online class without leaving the comfort of your bedroom. Some classes are offered free, while others charge. The price can range from a few bucks to hundreds of dollars.

Before we get into specifics, let me explain the difference between a writing class and a workshop. Some people may use the terms interchangeably, but they are not technically the same creature. In a writing class, you receive instruction and writing assignments. You are expected to complete your assignments, which may be evaluated by the instructor and/or other participants in the class.

In a workshop, participants work on a writing project that is already in progress. The information you learn as you go along can help you polish your work. You typically will also receive feedback from your instructor and/or other workshop participants.

Ideally, the instructor should also be a professional writer. After all, would you go to a mechanic to learn about brain surgery? I think not. Taking a class is a good way to get feedback on your work as well. I recently took an online poetry workshop, consisting of pre-recorded video lessons, and class assignments. Participants were required to upload several poems for critique by other classmates. At the end of the class, I felt confident enough to (finally) finish a collection of poems I was working on. The workshop helped me polish and refine my work. The collection was published in July 2016. Would I have finished and published my collection had I not taken the workshop? I don't think so.

But workshops and classes aren't for everyone. If you're interested, you should investigate classes that interest you before making a decision—especially if you're going to pay for it. You also have to decide if you can invest the necessary time in order to get the most from the class. If you enroll in a class or workshop but are not able to complete assignments, then you will not reap the full benefits.

As I write this chapter, I am taking an online (free!) writing class offered through the University of Iowa. The class runs six weeks and includes pre-recorded videos, class assignments, message boards, and private groups. After I signed up for the class, I realized I would not have time to complete the writing assignments or critique classmates. But, I still wanted to take advantage of the wealth of information. The alternative: I was able to audit the class. This allowed me to take the class without having to turn in assignments or critique others. Plus, I have access to the material for several months.

The length of a class or workshop may vary from one-day seminars to several weeks or months. If you aren't sure you can devote a large chunk of time, you should look for a one-day offering. Sometimes, these information-packed sessions may be what you need to get moving. I once took an all-day Saturday writing class at the University of South Alabama. I walked away with a ton of useful information. It was precisely what I needed at the time—and one day was all the time I had to spare.

Before deciding on a writing class, especially one where money changes hands, make sure you thoroughly research the sponsors. You also want to make sure the person teaching the class is qualified. When dealing with online classes, you definitely want to make sure the website is legitimate. In the appendix, you will find a list of reputable online and in-person writing classes and workshops.

Writing Groups

To be in the company of other writers is a beautiful thing. So when you decide to join this legion of wordsmiths, the next step is to hook up with a local (or virtual) writing group, right? *Bzzzzzt*—not so fast.

Like writing classes and workshops, writing groups are useful to some, but they can be a distraction (or total waste of time) to others. Most writing groups offer members the chance to share their work and receive feedback—or at least encouragement. The problem for some writers is they may take this feedback and completely revamp their work-in-progress based on the opinions of others.

They may suggest you move the plot in a direction you didn't want to go. Pointing out factual errors or inconsistencies is one thing. Telling a writer that he or she should change the setting, character traits, or other oddball suggestions should be taken with a grain of salt.

Years ago, I was excited to hear that my local library was hosting a six-week writing group. I attended exactly **ONE** session. Why? First, the moderator had each participant tell a little about ourselves and what we were working on. No problem, except some people had diarrhea of the mouth while the clock ticked away.

There was a young lady who didn't want to share what she was working on, like it was top secret. Which is okay, but she actually seemed angry that the moderator asked about it. Hello! It's a writing group, how can we help you if you don't share?

The moderator had absolutely no control over the group. One woman (you know there's always *that* person) tried to monopolize the conversation. She kept butting in when others talked about *their* work. At the end of four *long* hours, I knew this group was going to be a hot mess. I figured I could spend four productive hours writing at home rather than driving across town just to get annoyed.

That was my experience. Don't let me discourage you from seeking out your own writing group. You may have a better experience. Even though my one and only experience was not right for me, it didn't leave a bad taste in my mouth for future writing groups. I would totally give it another shot if the opportunity presented itself.

If one writing group doesn't work out, you can always try another.

How to evaluate a writing group

When evaluating a writing group, there are a few things to keep in mind before you decide to join.

Structure: When you meet with your writing group, the main focus should be writing, not socializing. It's okay to chat before or after the meeting, but you shouldn't waste time during the session gabbing about non-writing issues. It's important to evaluate how the group is structured to determine if you'll fit in.

You also want to make sure that the person in charge can handle the group. The moderator's job is to assure a smooth operation. It may take more than one person to handle all of the business of running a group, but there definitely has to be someone in charge. This includes responding to questions about the group, orientating new members, event planning, dissemination of information to current members, etc. If possible, attend a few meetings before making a decision. This way, you can peep in on what goes on before you commit.

Genre: Some groups focus on a particular genre, like romance writing, while others welcome writers from all genres. You may feel more at home with genre-specific writers, or you might feel equally as comfortable with different writers from various genres.

Membership: Some groups welcome any new member interested in joining, while others only accept members that are nominated by current members, or based on other criteria. Some groups, for instance, may limit the number of members so that the group remains small and intimate. They will only open membership to new applicants when a current member leaves the group.

Logistics: How often will the group meet, for how long, and where? You want a group that has a definite meeting plan. You don't want a group that "plays it by ear." Even if the group alternates the meeting location and dates, some type of plan should be decided in advance. For instance, if the group meets weekly but at different locations, a schedule should be planned at least several weeks ahead. You don't want to wait until the end of the session to decide the location of the next meeting.

Critique: A very important matter is whether the group will critique members' work, or simply share work-in-progress. What's your preference? If it's not in line with the group's mission, you may need to keep looking.

Mission: Speaking of mission—in addition to the issue of critiquing, you need to know the overall mission of the group before you join. The mission could include meeting to offer support, share resources, provide training, or a combination of these and other factors. Some groups may use a portion of their time together to actually write, while others simply share what they have worked on the preceding week(s).

Ultimately, if you plan to spend a lot of time with your writing group, you need to make sure it meets your needs.

Keeping a Writer's Notebook or Journal

The best writing advice I received was that I should keep a writing notebook. So, I'm passing that gem of wisdom on to you. I use a one-subject spiral notebook to jot down ideas, clever phrases, new words I discover, bits and pieces of dialogue I overhear, etc. Occasionally, these tidbits make their way into my writing projects. I created many poems for my collection from tidbits found in my writing journal. Many of these morsels have found their way into articles and blog posts I have written as part of my freelance writing business.

Some writers also use journals or diaries. That's cool. I have tried to use a journal to write down my thoughts at the end of the day about things that happened to me, but it was a bit time-consuming, and I was never able to write consistently. I like the writer's notebook because I jot things down as they occur.

If I don't have my notebook with me and inspiration hits, I whip out my phone and use the notebook app. I have even written stuff on the back of receipts, napkins, my hand . . . just kidding, don't write on your hands. Then, I transfer the information when I get home.

Author Ralph Fletcher writes: "My notebook is a potpourri of life-stuff, full of anecdotes, off-beat experiences, irritations, dreams, ideas for poems and books, worries, speculations, and goals."[19] Mine is the same. Bits and

---

19. Fletcher, 2015.

pieces of random thoughts that may never see the light of publication. But you never know.

Some writers buy fancy, shmancy, lamb-covered writing journals that are etched in gold. I prefer the cheap, dollar store variety. Because they are so cheap, I can buy a ton of them to use throughout the year. Over the years, I have bought more expensive ones (or received as gifts) but I always feel funny writing in them. I feel like if I use a fancy journal, whatever I write must be Pulitzer Prize-worthy.

The best time to snag a deal on notebooks is during the back-to-school rush. When my son was younger (he is a teen now and doesn't need the copious amount of school supplies required in elementary and middle school) I would grab a few extra notebooks for myself when I shopped for school supplies. I also find that drugstores like Walgreens and Rite Aid will often have quirky-covered notebooks on sale. When they do, I snag a few of them and hide them away in my desk drawer. Author Natalie Goldberg buys the same kinds of cheap notebooks that I do. In *Writing Down the Bones,* she writes that she uses the cheap spiral notebooks, which allow her to write ". . . the worst junk in the world and it would be okay."[20]

Goldberg also buys notebooks with funny characters like Garfield and the Muppets. She says she can't ". . . take herself too seriously when [she opens] up a Peanuts notebook."[21]

So what should you write in your notebook? Whatever random thoughts you want to jot down. I actually use two notebooks at all times. One contains only words that I like: either newly discovered words or words that pop into my head and make me smile. The second notebook contains random thoughts (I actually write 'RANDOM THOUGHTS' in a permanent marker on the outside cover). A sentence or phrase may pop into my head that sounds like it has potential. Or I may overhear a snippet of a conversation that sounds like it may be useful. It could be a fragment of a thought. Whatever it is, if I feel there's potential, I write it in my notebook.

Here are some examples from my writer's notebook:

Words I like (action words):

- Whoosh

- Gooey

- Slurp

- Plop

---

20. Goldberg, 1986.
21. Goldberg, 1986.

- Thwack

- Mmmmmm

Random thoughts:

- Just right weather (later used in a poem)

- Burst open like a case of explosive diarrhea (later used in a short story)

- Technological hiccup (later used in an article)

- Crumb-covered face (a description of my son when he was five; used in an essay)

- A chicken and egg situation (used in a short story I'm working on)

- He had a head like a 60-watt light bulb (contemplating using it in a novella I'm editing)

- A gritty whisper

- A prickly snort from a writing exercise (haven't used yet, but I will)

- A velvety giggle

- Colors: celery green; pumpkin orange; mayonnaise white (snipped from my son—he later gave me permission to use)

- My hair smells like coconut (well it does)

Snippets of eavesdropped overheard dialogue:

- "Oh, oh, oh now I get it!"

- "She's been that way since birth."

- "Do y'all ever do art shows out here? Because I do tattoos that look like art. They last for about two weeks."

- "That's a little more information than I wanted my children to know."

- "The part is bad," she screamed into her cellphone. "Would I be telling you I need the part if the part wasn't bad?" (overheard while waiting to get a new battery for my car)

- "Did you see that top she was wearing?"

I get some of my best ideas for my notebook by ~~eavesdropping on~~ *listening* to people. I think the secret to being a good writer is to be ~~nosey~~ *inquisitive*. Writing authentic dialogue is particularly hard for many new writers. The answer? Go out amongst the people, take your notebook (or laptop), and listen to real conversations.

Now, make sure you aren't too obvious. Seriously. Do not sit next to someone at Starbucks and lean into their conversation and ask: "Um, could you repeat that?"

But, there are ways to covertly listen without appearing to listen. I find that people talk so loud today that it's really easy to overhear conversations. I was in the dollar store just yesterday, and a lady was on her cellphone talking so loud that at first I thought she was talking to someone in the store. Then, I realized she was yelling into the phone. It was so loud and distracting I literally couldn't remember what I came in the store for. She walked around the store, completely oblivious to how loud she was talking.

Anyway, besides coffeehouses, I find libraries are good places to eavesdrop. Public transportation, stores, and restaurants are also very good bets.

Dealing with Writer's Block

Writer's Block. No two words strike more fear in the hearts of writers. Like rejection, writer's block happens to the best of us. But, it's not a death sentence or the end of the world. It is simply a **temporary** inability to proceed with a work in progress or create new work. Notice temporary is underlined and in bold print. This is what I want you to focus on. Like a bad case of acne (and the cafeteria mystery casserole you had for lunch) — this too shall pass.

In the *Writer's Encyclopedia*, readers are encouraged to perform work-related tasks during periods of blockage. This may include tidying up your desk or corresponding with other writers.

Further, the *Writer's Encyclopedia* asserts that in some cases, writer's block for some authors ". . . results from fear that their writing isn't any good, and once it's in print *other* people will see it and realize it's no good."[22]

---

22. Writer's Digest, 1996.

Robert Masello writes in *Robert's Rules of Writing,* that writer's block is not always a bad thing. He explains that when you hit a brick wall and you aren't sure where to go next in your narrative, ". . . then maybe your reader isn't sure either."[23]

Masello believes that a block may mean your work is crying out for something dramatic to happen. Instead of coming to a complete stop and feeling frustrated, the writer should simply slow down and use this time to discover the next direction your narrative should take. Masello also echoes the sentiments expressed in *Writer's Encyclopedia.* If an author is unable to begin writing, Masello thinks these are deeper issues usually related to feelings of self-worth.

In *The Craft & Business of Writing,* Anthony Tedesco lists five possible causes of writer's block: self-doubt, perfectionism, ill-suited subject or genre, fatalistic career outlook, and poor time management.

Most of these causes are self-explanatory, but let's take a closer look at two: ill-suited subject or genre and fatalistic career outlook.

Some writers attack subject matter or genres based on popularity or because other people have recommended they should. However, if it's not your passion, you're going to have trouble writing. After the success of Stephenie Meyer's *Twilight* series, it seems like everybody and their mama wanted to write about vampires. Look, I enjoy a good vampire story as much as the next guy, but I would probably never write a vampire story. I don't feel any *oomph* for writing in this genre. Same goes for subject matter. Being primarily a non-fiction writer, I can write about many subjects because I am a good researcher. But, there are subjects I would not be able to cover with the same enthusiasm, because I would find myself bored to tears.

---

23. Masello, 2005.

Unless you're already under contract, if you find yourself with a bad case of writer's block, it may be time to decide if your subject or genre is the cause of the obstruction.

The next issue is fatalistic career outlook. Sounds ominous, right? In this scenario, a writer is unable to write because he or she has received too many rejections. Remember: writers get rejected. Most are able to bounce back, even after multiple failures trying to place the same manuscript. Fatalists, on the other hand, may adopt a *what's the use* attitude.

Tedesco offers several useful tips on how to get past writer's block. Here are a few examples:

- **Fight negative with positive:** As pointed out, one of the reasons for writer's block is the belief that your work isn't good enough. If you can counter those negative thoughts with positive affirmations, you may be able to get the creative juices flowing.

- **Freewrite:** Tedesco says anything that gets you writing can stimulate the creative writing process, "Whether it's a grocery list or your favorite writing prompt . . ."[24]

- **Start in the middle:** Many writers labor over the first sentence. If they are unable to get it exactly perfect, some can't move on. Whenever I sit down to write, if the first sentence comes to me, good. If not, I always keep it moving. After all, I realize that I can return to the page later when that first line comes to me. Realizing that you can do the same can help eliminate writer's block.

- **Write badly:** Many writers feel the first draft has to be perfect. This can cause them to avoid moving forward after a bad writing session.

---

24. Tedesco, 2008.

Most accomplished writers will tell you that the first (bad) draft doesn't matter. Editing is what's important.

Another method of dealing with writer's block is to write less. This may seem counter-intuitive, but it makes a lot of sense. Forcing yourself to stare at a blank page (or computer screen) can cause more stress and anxiety, increasing the odds that your creative juices will temporary stop flowing. So go ahead and take a breather.

In the November/December 2006 issue of *Writer's Digest*, Michael J. Vaughn calls this break, "creative lollygagging." Lollygagging is an old-fashioned way of saying goofing off or hanging out without any apparent purpose. Examples of creative lollygagging, according to Vaughn, include:

- **Mobile activities** like biking, hiking or taking a long ride or train trip

- **Idle activities** like flying a kite, fly-fishing, or bowling solo

- **Engaging in boring jobs** like raking leaves, mowing the lawn, or even painting the garage

- **Dilettantism** which means dabbling in artistic pursuits like creating abstract paintings or making up tunes on the piano

If you plan to try the last activity, Vaughn notes this method only works if you try an activity in which you have no talent. Remember, the activity is supposed to give your mind a break, not potentially cause more stress.

Writing Resources

As a writer, you will not have to go it alone when you decide to publish your book; there are many resources available to help. You may have questions. Good, because this guide will provide you with answers. Let's take a look at some important issues that may be nagging you.

Where do I get ideas?

This is a question many new writers ask. They want to write, but they have concerns about where to find material to write about. Here are a few suggestions:

Your writer's notebook: Your trusty writer's notebook could hold a treasure trove of useful ideas, just waiting for you to develop them into full-fledged projects.

What if?: I watched an interview with master of horror, Stephen King, where he said that a lot of his stories sprang from a *what if?* scenario. In the "frequently asked questions" section of his website, **www.stephenking.com**, he elaborates:

> "I get my ideas from everywhere. But what all of my ideas boil down to is seeing maybe one thing, but in a lot of cases it's seeing two things and having them come together in some new and interesting way, and then adding the question 'What if?' 'What if' is always the key question."

Writing prompts: You can find great ideas using writing prompts, found either online or in print. You can find several resources for writing prompts in the appendix of this guide. Writing prompts are also often used in writing contests. Sites like **www.thefirstline.com**, hold quarterly contests where participants are giving the first line as a writing prompt and then they take it from there. It is interesting to read the different directions writers take after starting at the same point. Although the contest for the Fall

2016 has closed, why not give it a shot? Here's the prompt: Mrs. Morrison was too busy to die.

Use pictures as writing prompts: Sometimes, an idea may spring from a visual prompt rather than a written one. So, instead of taking endless selfies (after all, how many pictures do you really need of yourself?), use your camera to snap unusual or even mundane images. You never know when one may spark an idea. I have a picture of an old, rusty gas pump from the 1970s. I'm not sure how I'm going to use it, but I specifically took the picture because I thought it would make a nice writing prompt.

Adapting a public domain work: Any published work that is no longer under copyright protection is up for grabs. You can take an old fairy tale, for example, and give it a modern day twist.

Using a random plot generator: You may have heard about name generators. Some authors use them to create names for their characters. Non-writers use them to create online usernames. You can find also plot generators if you're stuck coming up with ideas. Remember, generators are random, so you could get a few wacky plot lines. Some plots may not make any sense at all, but who knows? You may be able to adapt the idea. Here's a few samples I found using different generators:

- A cheerleader borrows a diary. The circumstances are made difficult by a ticking bomb.

- A gifted policeman is ostracized for blackmail.

- A schoolgirl cross dresses as a happy-go-lucky mummy. The circumstances are worsened by a disaster.

- A bounty hunter and a flirtatious balloonist discover their true selves in a pastry shop.

Writing software

Many writers turn to writing software when working on their books. You certainly do not *need* writing software—most word processing programs will work fine. The main reason to buy writing software (according to companies that produce them) is to help you stay organized while you write.

Many writers swear by Scrivener as their software of choice. It offers tools like an outliner and a virtual corkboard where you can stick little index cards with notes on it. I am all for tools that will help me write better, but at 50 bucks (although you can often catch the software on sale), I will stick with Microsoft Word.

If you're curious, you can usually download and try most software for free for a limited time. The appendix lists contact information for some of the more popular writing software programs on the market.

If you're looking for a free option, try Evernote. It has many useful and powerful tools. Did I mention . . . it's free?

Should you join a professional writing association?

Professional writing organizations are useful for writers no matter where you are in your career. Here are some ways joining a writing association can help:

- You have the chance to connect with other writers

- Many offer members-only perks and training opportunities

- Shows others you are committed to writing

- It's a great way to connect with editors and literary agents

- Some offer members only contests and awards

- Some offer job boards or post information on publishers actively seeking manuscripts

Many associations have national and local chapters. Local affiliates give you the chance for face-to-face networking with your fellow writers. Associations typically have annual conventions or other special events.

You can join an association that accepts writers from all genres, or you can choose a genre-specific group like the Mystery Writers of America. There are associations for children's writers, Christian novelists, military writers, freelance writers and more. You will need to check the organization's membership information to determine if you meet the criteria. Some require members to have published a book already, while others are open to unpublished writers.

Some associations offer different membership levels including membership for students. Dues vary; expect to pay $50 or more for an annual membership. The appendix lists some of the more popular writers' associations.

National novel writing month (NaNoWriMo) young writers program

Can you write a novel in one month? That is the goal each November as thousands of professional and aspiring writers pledge to write a novel in thirty days. Don't worry, it's a first draft, so you can silence your inner critic while you pound out your creation.

The Young Writers Program is an offshoot of the adult challenge. The goal is the same — to write a novel in one month.

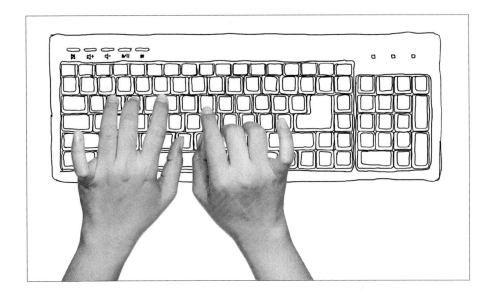

Participating is easy. Here's what you need to do:

Sign up for an account: You will need an adult (parent, guardian, teacher) to review the terms and conditions, and to give you permission to participate.

Create a profile: Complete the profile, giving out as much (or as little) information as you feel comfortable sharing. You can also upload an image.

Start writing: From your dashboard, fill in information on your writing project and set your word count goal. In the adult challenge, participants must set a minimum goal of 50,000 words. Young writers can set any goal they want.

You can write your novel directly into the space provided on the website, or in your favorite word processing program. If you write on the site, it will automatically update your daily word count. If you're using an offline program, you will have to manually update each day, or you can wait to the end of the challenge to load your work.

Participants have access to other features including a tool for writing notes, writing challenges and prompts, resources, forums, and pep talks. If you're interested in participating in the next challenge, check out their website for more information: **https://ywp.nanowrimo.org**.

Create Your Own Writing Marathon

You can create your own mini writing marathons. You can ask a fellow writer to join you, or go solo. The point is to set aside a specific amount of time to write. No TVs, social media, cell phones or other distractions. Just write.

You can write for a few hours or for an entire day. Even as a full-time writer, I often carve out time for mini write-a-thons, where I work on new (or on-going) creative pieces.

Writing partners

Batman and Robin. Bert and Ernie. Peanut Butter and Jelly. Hey, sometimes you need a partner, and writing is no exception. If you work well with others, this may be a viable option for you.

A writing partner can be beneficial because it will take some of the pressure off you. As the saying goes: "Two heads are better than one."

With a writing partner, you can bounce ideas off each other. If one of you has an off day, the other can pick up the slack. The important thing to consider is whether the two of you work well together and have the same writing style. Most importantly, you need to decide in advance the exact plan for writing your book. You can't simply sit down and start writing. Will you alternate chapters? Will one person write and the second person edit the same chapter? These are the types of questions you need to answer *before* you start writing.

Bestselling author Walter Dean Meyers writes in *Just Write: Here's How!* that having a co-author can be worthwhile for both authors. But he admits it may not work for everyone. For example, his first attempt ended a friendship with a close friend, who accused him of being ". . . an egomaniac, a rotter, and a know-it-all."[25]

A second effort didn't go as planned, either. Meyers was supposed to do most of the writing, while his pal did the majority of the research. Meyers ended up doing most of the research, too. So, even with the best-conceived plans, things still may not go as planned. But, the show must go on. There is good news, though. In 2011, Meyers successfully published a book, *Kick*, coauthored with Ross Workman.

First readers

You have done the hard work. Congratulations, the first draft of your book is complete. Now what? Before sending a complete manuscript off to the publisher, some writers have first readers review their work.

Even master writers like Stephen King have a first reader (his wife Tabitha). In *On Writing: A Memoir of the Craft*, King says when he writes, he has an ideal reader in mind. He wonders what this person will think about certain parts of his books. In this case, his wife is the person he has in mind, and she is the one he turns to when his manuscript is complete.

King writes that his wife is a sympathetic and supportive first reader, but she doesn't hesitate to point out potential issues. "When she does, she lets me know loud and clear," King writes.[26]

---

25. Meyers, 2012
26. King, 2010

King also says he sends his manuscript out to between four and eight first readers that have read his work over the years. But, ultimately, the decision about whether you want to use a first reader or not is totally up to you.

Choosing a Title

Choosing a book title can cause the same amount of anxiety to some authors as writing that first line. But it doesn't have to be that way. It is perfectly OK to write a book without knowing the title. You can label it "*Untitled,*" "*Work in Progress,*" or "*Whatever.*"

Go ahead and start writing; the title will come to you eventually. Keep in mind: an editor or publisher may change the title of your book anyway. Unless you self-publish, I would not obsess over your book's title.

According to the *Writer's Encyclopedia*, "The important elements of good titles are clarity and suspense."[27] The title should hint at what the book is

27. Writer's Digest, 1996

about but not give away all its secrets. Although sometimes even accomplished writers don't follow this rule. I refuse to call names, but one of my favorite writers recently published a book that had a lot of fans annoyed. Why? The title pretty much gave away the ending of the book. Of course, in order to tip off readers, prior knowledge of the phrase was needed. Unfortunately, quite of few fans knew the phrase and thus predicted the outcome of the story. So, please make sure you don't give away your book's ending in the title.

In *The Essential Guide to Getting Your Book Published,* Eckstut and Sterry write that your title should make a reader want to, ". . . pick up your book, buy it and read it."[28] Also, nonfiction books should clearly convey what the book is about. The authors also point out that one mistake writers often make is choosing a title that means something to them but leaves readers scratching their heads. While you may think your title is clever, readers (and potential buyers) are left feeling confused as they place your book back on the shelf and move on to the next author.

Here are a few tips on choosing a title for your book:

Run an Internet Search: You want your title to be original. You can easily find out by running an Internet search. While you cannot copyright a title, it is best to choose an original title to avoid confusion. Potential readers will get angry at you if you purposely try to mislead them by choosing a title similar to another well-known book.

Random Book Generators: Yes, random generators are everywhere. In addition to using a generator when you need a plot idea, you can also use one to find your standout book title. Good idea? You be the judge. Here are some titles I created from different generators:

---

28. Eckstut and Sterry, 2010

Burning Children

Alexander, The Black Slab

The Woodcarver's Escape

Mindless

Card Dragging

The Punch Dome

Smooth Eyes

The Alien's Boyfriend

The Broken Man

The Door of the Snake

Roses in the Shadow

The Forgotten School

The Wet Light

Years of Elves

The Words of the Moon

Allow the Title to Find You: It has already been established that you don't need a title to begin writing. It's fine to have a "working title" that you can change later, or title your manuscript "*Untitled Work-in-Progress December 2016.*" Sometimes, as you write, a line or phrase will jump out and smack you across the face. Voilà — now you have a great title for your book. When I am reading fiction, I always make a game to find the line in the book where the title sprang from, if applicable.

Just remember that along with the cover design, your title will determine if a potential reader is motivated to pick up your book. You want a title that grabs the reader by the collar and says, "Go ahead, read me. I know you want to." The title should be one that readers will remember (and recommend to others). Although I have read a lot of good books, the ones I seem to remember are the ones with memorable titles. You don't want people fumbling around trying to remember the name of your book, so make it memorable.

Do You Need a Subtitle?

Most fiction books will not require a subtitle. For non-fiction, if the title is ambiguous, you may need to add a subtitle to avoid confusion. The title should intrigue or hook the reader to want to know more. The subtitle explains the premise of the book and hopefully reels the reader in.

Best Book Titles

These gems made the list of 100 best book titles as voted by readers on Goodreads.com:

1. *I Was Told There'd Be Cake* by Sloane Crosley

2. *The Hollow Chocolate Bunnies of the Apocalypse (Eddie Bear #1)* by Robert Rankin

3. *The Earth, My Butt, and Other Big Round Things* by Carolyn Mackler

4. *Me Talk Pretty One Day* by David Sedaris

5. *Alexander and the Terrible, Horrible, No Good, Very Bad Day* by Judith Viorst

6. *When Will Jesus Bring the Pork Chops?* by George Carlin

7. *The Man Who Was Thursday: A Nightmare* by G.K. Chesterton

8. *The Catcher in the Rye* by J.D. Salinger

9. *Nostradamus Ate My Hamster* by Robert Rankin

10. *Don't Pee on My Leg and Tell Me It's Raining: America's Toughest Family Court Judge Speaks Out* by Judy Sheindlin, Josh Getlin

Here are some favorite titles from my own book shelf:

1. *The Beast*, by Walter Dean Meyer

2. *Split Images*, by Elmore Leonard

3. *Opposable Thumbs*, by Suzanne Hudson

4. *At the Mountain of Madness*, by H.P. Lovecraft

Dipping Your Feet in the Writing Pool Before Jumping In

Before you commit to spending months, years even, writing and publishing a book, you may want to test the water first. Let's look at a few ways you can do this.

Blogging

One way to commit to a set writing schedule to see if you have the writing chops necessary to complete a book is to start your own blog, or find a paid blog opportunity. A blog is a smash up of two words: **web + log**. In the early days of blogging, much of the content was political commentary. Eventually, these online diaries appealed to individuals, and pretty soon, it seemed like everybody on the Internet had a blog.

Today, we have corporate blogs, political blogs, personal blogs, microblogs—blogs have even replaced websites for many individuals and businesses as their primary online presence.

So, should you blog? Blogs can be useful or a waste of time. The ease in setting up a blog is why many people jump in without considering the time and effort it takes to maintain one and grow your readership.

Blogging could potentially help your writing career. Let's look at a scenario:

Suppose you decide to write a nonfiction book. But first, you decide to start a blog on the subject. After a lot of hard work, you create a loyal following. You are churning out blog posts like nobody's business, and the comments section flows with accolades.

At this point, you have a built-in audience. If you publish a book on the same subject, you can expect some (if not all) of your followers to purchase it.

If you're lucky, you could get a book deal *and* a movie from your blog. It happened to Julie Powell, who after blogging about cooking her way through a Julia Child cookbook garnered such a huge following that she subsequently received a publishing deal with Little, Brown and Company. Her book, *Julie & Julia: 365 Days, 524 Recipes, 1 Tiny Apartment Kitchen,* was published in 2005, but Powell's good fortune did not stop there. The book was made into the 2009 movie, *Julie & Julia,* starring Amy Adams as Powell and Meryl Streep as Julia Child.

Freelancing

If you want to see if you have what it takes to be a writer *and* make money while doing so, considering freelancing. There are many opportunities available for freelancers—some of which aren't age-restrictive.

Let's make sure we're all on the same page. Dictionary.com defines free-lancer as: "a person who works as a writer, designer, performer, or the like, selling work or services by the hour, day, job, etc., rather than working on a regular salary basis for one employer."[29]

I am a freelancer. I work full-time, at home writing for . . . well . . . frankly, anyone that will pay me. Freelancing is a good way to learn to meet dead-lines. If you blog for yourself, you have the option of writing on your own schedule. If you are disciplined, this could work well for you.

When you accept a freelance assignment, you will have a deadline, and an editor will expect you to turn your work in on time. Freelancing could also help you learn to deal with rejection and criticism. You will need both traits as a writer.

Magazines, websites, newspapers, and businesses all use freelancers for writing projects. If you have a knack for writing and can produce great content, you can probably find freelance work. You can find work by checking job boards or by querying publications you would like to work for. The appendix includes resources for finding freelance opportunities.

---

29. **www.dictionary.com**, 2016.

CASE STUDY: JESSICA PIPER

"I started getting paid to write when I was 18," Jessica says. "I thought it would be great if I could have the chance to make money doing something I liked so much."

She encourages young writers to make sure they are OK with the level of compensation they are receiving for their service. "Especially when you are young, people may try to pay you very little or take advantage of you in other ways," she says."In the writing world, many places ask you to write but won't pay you—they say you benefit from the 'exposure.' If you are starting your own business, you probably want to get paid. Make sure you are working with people who recognize this goal and value your time and energy."

In addition to writing for her college newspaper, Jessica found freelance writing opportunities by scanning job boards.

"My first book got published when I was 19," she says. "I remember receiving six copies from my publisher and being amazed to see my own name on the front cover!"

Jessica says she likes to tell people to search her name on Amazon, where they'll see her listed as an author. As a full time college student, she finds the scheduling flexibility of freelance writing works better for her than a part time job, and she gets to do something she loves.

"My biggest piece of advice is don't underestimate yourself. It's easy to think 'I'm not qualified,' but you probably are. In the real world, people often judge you on your abilities – not your age or your level of education. If you have a skill or talent that other people would appreciate, go for it!"

Jessica enjoys writing about obscure historical happenings, contemporary social issues, and analysis of popular culture. You can find her on Twitter @jsscppr.

Contests

Another way to flex your writing muscles is to enter contests. Again, many writing contests are open to individuals of all age groups. A careful reading of the contest rules will enlighten you. If in doubt, call or email the contest sponsors for clarification.

There are also many writing contests that are specifically aimed at teens and young adults. Many of the contests are essay writing, but some are open to poems and fiction genres.

Contests offer great opportunities to see your work in print and earn money. But, there are scams that target writers, so be careful. Many will take your money (in the form of an entry fee) and skedaddle without paying out a single penny. Be cautious and check out the sponsor before you enter.

Many writers wonder if there are ways to increase their odds of winning a writing contest. Besides sending your best work, make sure to read the guidelines. If the guidelines call for a particular theme, genre or word count, follow the rules, or you will have no chance of winning.

A contest's guidelines will tell you how to format your entry. Again, follow the procedure, or you will get disqualified. For instance, some contests are judged "blind," meaning your name shouldn't appear on the actual manuscript, but on a separate cover letter instead.

It's a good idea to read the work of winners from previous contests. This will give you an idea of the type of work the sponsor looks for. Finally, it wouldn't hurt to read the work of the judges if you know who they are. If you are entering a poetry contest judged by poets, you can bet they will lean toward poems reminiscent of their own work.

Check the appendix for a list of reputable contests you can enter.

Copyright and Legal Issues

A big concern for writers involves theft of their creative work. There are laws to protect this from happening. It's called copyright.

Copyright is "the exclusive legal right to reproduce, publish, sell, or distribute the matter and form of something (as a literary, musical, or artistic work)."[30]

I cannot tell you how many people have expressed concern that an editor or publisher may nab their work. Relax, it rarely happens. Many writers wonder if they should register their work with the United States Copyright Office. Registering your work is not necessary to claim copyright. According to the copyright office: "Your work is under copyright protection the moment it is created and fixed in a tangible form that it is perceptible either directly or with the aid of a machine or device."[31]

In other words, as soon as you create your masterpiece, it is under copyright protection. You may have heard you should mail a copy of your work (keep it sealed) to yourself. The postmark is supposed to serve as proof that you created the work on a particular date.

This is called a "poor man's copyright." According to the copyright office, "There is no provision in the copyright law regarding any such type of pro-

---

30. **www.merriam-webster.com**, 2016.
31. **www.copyright.gov**, 2016.

tection, and it is not a substitute for registration."[32] Again, it is rare that an editor or publisher would steal your manuscript and publish it under another author. But, keep in mind that it is possible that you may submit an idea to a publisher who already has a similar idea under contract. If you think your idea was filched, you would have to prove overwhelming similarities to your work and the work in question.

As for published books, if you self-publish and want to secure copyright for your book, the current fee for a single application filed online is $35. A traditional publisher will handle the copyright process for you.

Editing and Revising

To write means to edit and revise. In a perfect world, we writers would churn out wonderful first drafts that would bring editors to tears. But we do not live in a perfect world, and most of us have to edit our work. Or as the *Writer's Encyclopedia* so elegantly proclaimed: ". . . every piece of writing will not be a masterpiece."[33]

Whole books are devoted to editing and revising techniques. The appendix will list some of the more popular ones to add to your writing resource library. For now, here are some important tips to keep in mind when editing and revising your manuscript.

Revision tips

1. **Be specific**: When editing your work, go back over what you have written to see if you can add more punch by being more specific. For example, Natalie Goldberg in *Writing Down the Bones*, says instead of writing "fruit,"

---

32. **www.copyright.gov**.
33. Writer's Digest, 1996.

tell what type of fruit it is. Likewise, if you write about a flower in the window, change your description to a specific flower. These small changes help the reader gain a better picture of the scene the writer is imagining.

2. **Showing versus telling:** Writers often use narrative summary to describe to readers what is taking place in a story. It is a better idea to set the scene with just enough information so that readers can picture it for themselves.

There are times when you may have to use narrative summary, write Renni Brown and Dave King in *Self-editing for Fiction Writers: How to Edit Yourself into Print*. For instance, when writing a historical novel or science fiction, the authors point out that both genres usually require a lot of explanatory information the readers will need before the material touches them emotionally. Brown and King also point out that the "show, don't tell" rule is not etched in stone. "There are going to be times when telling will create more engagement than showing," they write.[34]

3. **Writing dialogue:** For new (and some seasoned) fiction writers, crafting dialogue is often something they struggle with. It can be difficult to write dialogue that doesn't sound stiff. As pointed out earlier, a good technique that will help you learn to write believable dialogue is to really listen to the way people speak to each other. A big issue for writers is what Brown and King describe as the need for writers to explain. As an example, they use this sentence:

"You can't be serious," she said in astonishment. [35]

The sentence alone conveys a sense of astonishment, so there's no need for further explanation. The authors write that if you explain your dialogue when no explanation is needed, you risk turning your readers off. It is also patronizing. They suggest if you feel like you have to explain you should remember to R.U.E. — **R**esist the **U**rge to **E**xplain.

4. **Read your work aloud:** This may seem like a chore, but reading your work aloud — Every. Single. Word. — will help you determine if your story flows as it should. As an alternative, enlist the aid of a friend or family member to read your story aloud to you. Most writers hear a specific voice when they are writing. Having someone else read your work aloud allows you to imagine how your reader hears the story. A final option is to use a text-to-speech software program that will read your manuscript. The problem with this type of software is the voices often sound robotic — which they are. Some programs have more naturally-sounded readers, but nothing takes the place of a real person.

---

34. Brown and King, 2004.
35. Brown and King, 2004.

5. Distance makes the heart grow fonder: When you spend so much time writing and then revising your manuscript, there may come a point when you notice that all of your words *startrunningtogetherlikethis.* Or worse, you start over editing, lamenting on every word and sentence. The solution? Step back from your finished draft and take a breather. When you return with fresh eyes, you will be better equipped to smooth out any rough edges in your manuscript and finish strong.

6. Write in your own voice: Writers often feel they need to write with a thesaurus near, ready to grab a more grandiose word than the one they have just written. You will impress no one with your big words. Take the words of Mark Twain to heart: "Don't use a five-dollar word when a fifty-cent word will do." So put away your thesaurus and your fancy big words. In *Robert's Rule of Writing,* Robert Masello points out that words found in a thesaurus are words you would never use on your own. "They aren't words that come readily to your mind or rest comfortably in your working vocabulary."[36]

The words will feel out of place if you put them in the mouths of someone who would never utter those words in the real world. There are exceptions. If the character is supposed to be a pompous know-it-all, then it's possible he would use $5 or even $10 words. Especially when talking to characters he considers intellectually inferior. As Masello writes, you should use words that you already know, not ones you have borrowed specifically for your story.

7. Embrace the revision process: Many writers dislike the revision process. Don't be that writer. Instead, you should embrace this method of fine-tuning your work. Yes, it can be a bit tedious, but in the end, your manuscript will sparkle if you take the time to look for areas in your man-

---

36. Masello, 2005.

uscript that need improvement. In *Just Write: Here's How,* Walter Dean Meyers writes that some authors do not like the revision process ". . . because it ruins the spontaneity of their work."[37] Meyers says writers shouldn't be too hard on themselves during the revision process. It should be fun, not a chore.

8. **Write your first draft without outside interference:** The impulse to share your work as you write is strong. Resist it. It is better to write a completed first draft of your work without any outside interference. Why? Because feedback or questions from the person you share your work with can stop you dead in your tracks or throw you off course.

We have covered a lot of territory in this chapter. I know you are anxious to start writing, so let's talk next about an important subject—the publishing process.

---

37. Meyers, 2012.

Chapter 3: *Go*

Chapters 1 and 2 provided you with the framework to get started on your publishing adventure. In this important chapter, we discuss the important task of getting your masterpiece into the hands of readers. Let's talk about publishing.

At this point, you may have already decided which publishing route—self or traditional—you will take. If not, don't worry. There's still time to decide. This chapter is a crash course of the basics of publishing. Let's get started.

How Traditional Publishing Works

If you plan to approach a major publisher, you will probably need a literary agent. There is more about literary agents in Chapter 5, but for now keep in mind that many publishers will not consider your manuscript unless it is submitted through an agent. The good news is some publishers will accept unagented material. A quick search of the publisher's website will confirm if they accept manuscripts directly from the author. The submission guidelines will also specify the process for submission. This is very important, because publishers' submission guidelines vary. Publisher "A" may request two sample chapters, while publisher "B" may want three. Publisher "C," on the other hand, may want the complete manuscript. So, it is important to read the guidelines carefully and send only what is requested.

Okay, so you've read the guidelines, and you're ready to submit your work. Here's a quick rundown of what happens next.

Your agent (or you) will submit your manuscript, per the guidelines. For fiction and narrative non-fiction titles, as stated above, you may have to submit a few chapters or a complete manuscript. For non-fiction work, expect to submit a book proposal, outline, and sample chapters. Again, the number of sample chapters will vary.

Next, an editorial team will review your manuscript or non-fiction proposal. They will scrutinize every word of your submission package. A committee — usually consisting of editors, production staff, sales representatives, in-house publicists, and sometimes the publisher or owner — will decide if your manuscript or proposal is worth pursuing. If so, they will offer you a contract.

Publishers receive oodles of manuscripts each month. Although it may seem like the default answer is "no," publishers are hopeful they will find that one perfect gem in the huge mound of manuscripts known as the slush pile.

Here are some of the factors they will consider as they pour over your submission:

- **The quality of your writing:** They will evaluate how well your words flow across the page. The committee will also evaluate how much editing may be required to get your work publication-ready.

- **Is this idea marketable?:** Just because you think your idea has potential does not make it so. A publisher will have to consider if readers will actually want to buy the book.

- **Your ability to promote and publicize your book:** Writers are often surprised that they are expected to promote their own book. Although publishers have marketing teams, authors are expected to help publicize their book. If the committee feels you lack the skills or the desire to help in promotion, your manuscript may not make it to print.

- **Will the book still be timely when printed?:** If you take the self-publishing route, you can have your book in the hands of readers quickly. The traditional route takes much longer. It may take a year or more before your book is published from the time you sign your contract. If your idea is time-sensitive, unless the publisher feels the book can reach the market quickly, they may pass on your idea.

- **Is there a large enough audience for this book?:** Niche markets are fine, but micro-niche markets — not so much. A publisher will not consider a book if the potential audience is too small.

- **Does the book have other sales potential?:** How many movies or television programs have you watched recently that are based on books? Probably a lot. When evaluating your idea, publishers will look at other sales avenues like film rights.

- **Is the market over-saturated with similar books?:** Readers eventually get sick of seeing the same types of books. I am a big fan of dystopian and time travel novels. I love old school classics like *The Giver* or *The Time Machine*. I am also a fan of recent novels like *11/22/63*, *The Hunger Games*, and the *Divergent* series. Although I love these books and similar titles, after reading so many of them, I often feel like I'm reading the same old stale plot. If your book idea is similar to many books already on the market, the publisher is likely to pass.

What Happens After You Get a Publishing Deal?

Once you land a publishing contract, take a moment to celebrate. Then, take a deep breath, because now the hard work begins. Even if you have submitted a complete manuscript, don't think you can sit back and wait for your book to be published and for the royalties to roll in. You will, most likely, have to fine-tune your manuscript. Let's take a closer look at what you can expect.

You will be expected to participate in:

- **Manuscript prep:** The first step in the process is preparing your book for publication. Your editor will work hard with you to make sure your book is publication-ready. It is an editor's job to edit, so please don't get bent out of shape if you're asked to change something in your manuscript. You may even have to "kill your darling" — remove elements from your manuscript that don't further the flow of your work. Your work will be copyedited for format, punctuation, spelling, grammar, word tense and usage, and syntactical errors. Your text is checked for potential issues, including copyrights, trademarks, permissions, citations, and libel. The editor will take care of copyright, International Standard Book Number (ISBN), and Library of Congress Control Number (CIP) registrations.

Here's what's happening behind the scenes:

- **Book design and sales:** The graphics department will get busy designing the layout and artwork for both the cover and interior of your book. The marketing department will write the sales copy. You may have noticed testimonials or review quotes on books you have read. The marketing department is responsible for these tasks.

- **Off to the printer:** Once the manuscript has been polished and edited until it shines, it's time for the next exciting phase of publishing — printing your book!

- **Create promotional material:** The marketing team will design and distribute sales items like posters, signs, fliers, and bookmarks. They also write cover letters to send to book reviewers and create advertising copy.

- **Market the book:** Once your book is printed, copies are usually sent to reviewers. Your publisher will also place ads in print magazines and online. Book tours and media may also be arranged. Publishers will also place your book in their catalogs to sell to book-dealers, libraries and others.

- **Distribution of your book:** Your publisher will fulfill all orders to major dealers, stores, and libraries.

Contract Basics

Congratulations! You just landed a publishing deal. Your publisher will offer you a contract. I know you are excited, but before you sign your name, you need to read through the contract thoroughly.

A book contract is a legal document that protects both you and the publisher. It clearly defines what is expected from both parties. Some of the language in the contract may sound foreign to you. If so, it's OK to question anything you don't understand. You can also have a lawyer or someone more familiar with contracts review it before you sign. If you have an agent, he or she will help you understand the terms of the contract. Here are some of the terms you will see on your contract.

Rights: When you land a book deal, you grant certain rights to the publisher. Specifically, you are giving them the go ahead to publish your work, in a particular format, and for a particular length of time. In exchange, they pay you for your rousing words.

Copyright: If you recall in Chapter 2, I gave you an overview of the copyright issue. When you snag a publishing deal, you will see a mention of copyright in your contract. As the author (unless you have some other type of deal) you are the copyright holder. The publisher may, however, include in your contract that they will take care of the necessary paperwork and file it for you.

Advance: You may have heard about authors landing six-figure book deals and receiving a huge advance. Maybe you're not exactly sure what an advance means. Let me explain. When you land a contract, your publisher will probably pay you a tidy sum of money. This amount is given to the writer in expectation for future earnings. It is also sort of a pre-payment for the many hours you are going to spend hammering out your masterpiece. The amount of the advance varies. You may not get an advance at all (especially for smaller publishing houses). You may get a few thousand dollars or be one of the lucky ones to get five figures.

A publisher may calculate the advance based on many factors including the perceived marketability of the book, the author's following, etc. Advances are typically split into three payments: a third when you sign your contract, another third when you turn in the completed manuscript, and the final third when the book is published. However, publishers have their own schedule of how they pay out advances.

Royalty: A royalty is the amount of money an author receives from the sale of a book. If your contract states you will receive a 10 percent royalty, and your book retails for $20, your royalty is $2 per book. Now, the bad news. Remember the advance you received? Until the publisher recoups the amount they have already paid to you through your advance, you will not receive a royalty check. So, in the above scenario, if you received an advance of $15,000, and you are earning royalties at the rate of $2 per book, you will need to sell enough books to cover the advance already paid to you. In this case, 7,500 books ($15,000 ÷ $2) before you receive any royalty checks. But there is also some good news: if you receive an advance but never sell enough books for the publisher to recoup those funds, you will not have to repay the advance. You simply will not receive a royalty. Royalties are paid at specific times as outlined in your contract.

21st Century Publishing

It's a great time to be a writer. With so many options available, anyone who wants to publish a book literally can. Writers have the option of trying to place their manuscript with a traditional publisher or take control of their work by self-publishing. Let's take a look at traditional publishing options first.

The Big Five

When I first started freelancing, like most writers, I wanted my byline to appear in the higher-paying, easily-recognized glossies. You know, the ones you see at the checkout stand or on the bookstore shelves. You see, no one told me the competition for these markets was stiff. So I aimed high. I was fortunate to have work accepted quickly, leading me to the false assumption that getting my work placed was always going to be easy peasy. But I was mistaken. I have been able to successfully make a living as a freelancer, howevermy work has appeared in markets of all sizes.

When most authors start looking for a publishing home for their book, they also aim high. They court the big publishing houses, specifically what's known in the publishing world as "the Big Five." Getting a deal with one of the Big Five announces to the world that you have arrived. But, as you can imagine, especially for new writers, snagging a book deal with one of these publishing giants is like finding a mythical unicorn hanging out in your backyard.

In the United States, the Big Five publishing houses are:

- Hachette Book Group

- HarperCollins

- MacMillan

- Penguin Random House

- Simon & Schuster

The Big Five was previously the Big Six until Random House and Penguin merged in 2013. Under the wings of each large publisher are imprints. An imprint is a segment of a publishing company that markets to a specific group of readers. For example, children's literature. Imprints are sometimes named after the editor. How cool is that?

You probably own books from the Big Five publisher or one of their imprints. Here are some imprints from the Big Five.

Hachette Book Group: *Little, Brown and Company, Jimmy Patterson, Little, Brown Books for Young Readers, Faith Words, Grand Central Publishing, Yen Press*

HarperCollins: *Amistad, Anthony Bourdain Books, HarperTeen, Blink, Harlequin Books, Walden Pond Press*

MacMillan: *Farrar, Straus and Giroux, Henry Holt & Co., Minotaur Books, Farrar, Straus and Giroux Books for Younger Readers, Tor Books, Holt Books for Young Readers*

Penguin Random House: *Books on Tape, DK, Putnam, Golden Books, Sylvan Learning, Alfred A. Knopf*

Simon & Schuster: *Pocket, Scribner, Simon & Shuster Books for Young Readers, Aladdin, Little Simon, Touchstone*

Fast Fact

Alexandra Adornetto landed a book deal with Big Five publisher HarperCollins when she was only 14. Adornetto, a native of Australia, published *The Shadow Thief* in 2007 under the HarperCollins Australia imprint. The group also purchased two more books in what would become the *Strangest Adventure* series. Adornetto–which is actually her pen name; her real name is Alexandra Grace–made her U.S. publishing debut with *Halo* (2010). This Young Adult fantasy romance book was the first in a three-book series published by another Big Five publisher–MacMillan.

Other Publishing Options

While it's fine to aim for a contract with one of the Big Five, they aren't the only kids on the playground. Be aware there are many other options available for placing your work. You will probably have a better chance of publishing your work through one of the following types of publishers.

University Presses: A university press is a publishing house connected to a college or university. They have been around for a gazillion years. Most people think since these presses are connected to the academic community, they only publish scholarly work or complex literary work. Today, most university presses publish work across all genres.

If your work has regional appeal, you may want to consider sending your manuscript to a university press in that particular region.

Fast Fact

John Hopkins University Press is the oldest press in the U.S. It was founded in 1878, two years after the school opened. The first book published was *Sidney Lanier: A Memorial Tribute*. It was published in 1881 to honor the university's first writer-in-residence. The press publishes 80 scholarly journals and about 200 books a year. Since 1993, it has been housed in a renovated former church, located in the Charles Village neighborhood of Boston.

There are hundreds of university presses where your manuscript may find a home. Like traditional publishers, you will need to carefully read the guidelines for each to make sure they accept the type of material you are interested in publishing. The Association of American University Presses (**www.aaupnet. org**) is a good place to begin your search. The site lists member information, complete with website, blog, and social media links. You can also check the website of universities in your city or region. Many university presses also offer contests, another opportunity to have your work published.

Small Presses: Most writers aspire to have their work published by one of the big publishing giants. But for new writers, submitting your work to a small press publisher may be a better option. What do I mean by small press?

Let's look at some typical traits of a small press.

- Small press = small budget. So, do not expect to get that big advance you have been dreaming about.

- Small presses are independently owned and are not part of a big publishing family.

- Small presses typically operate on funds secured through grants, donations, and the personal funds of the publisher.

- Small presses publish fewer books each year because of the lack of a fat publishing budget.

- A writer working with a small press is usually more involved in the publishing process than he or she would be when working with a larger publisher (editing, layout and book design, for example).

- Small presses typically will not have the budget to do large-scale marketing for your book and/or offer limited distribution.

- Making money is not the main goal of a small press; getting your book into the hands of readers who will appreciate it is.

Sounds like you should run from a small press. But wait—not so fast—a small press has advantages. If you are looking for a cozier relationship with your publisher, a small press is a good option. Because they publish fewer books each year, they have more time to spend with their writers.

In an article in *The Writer* (September, 2011), Elizabeth King Humphrey writes that a small press is a good option for authors who feel their work is strong but might not fit with bigger publishing houses. And as Michael Bourne pointed out in the November/December 2012 issue of *Poets & Writers*, "Unlike a mainstream press, where most editors are employees answering to executives of some distant corporation, an indie publisher has as much stake in the success or failure of a book as the author does."[38]

A small press can be the stepping stone that leads to bigger publishing deals. Before you set your sights on the Big Five, you owe it to yourself to see what a smaller press has to offer.

Self-Publishing: Self-publishing is no longer the redheaded stepchild of the publishing world. At one time, authors self-published because they couldn't get a deal from a traditional publisher. Today, many authors self-publish for many reasons. For example:

- Fewer books are being published by the big conglomerates, and even fewer by smaller publishers.

- Even if you get a book contract, the time from the closing of your deal to publication can take years. You can self-publish and get your book in the hands of readers in significantly less time.

- Authors retain more control over their work. The cost in publishing your book falls in your lap, but so does the majority of the profits.

CASE STUDY: MELISSA CARTER

My journey as a writer began when I was a child. I enjoyed writing projects in school, and in my teenage years my interest for poetry grew immensely. I was always very inspired by musical lyrics and loved the style of rhyming or the poetic meanings of the verses in songs.

In college, I took creative writing classes and in one class wrote over forty poems for my portfolio. When I decided to write my first book, that's just what I did. I said, "I want to write a children's book." While I didn't expose this to the world, internally I began thinking of ideas: a main character came about, along with the storyline. I knew I needed to search for an illustrator, and what about publishing? I had no experience in professional writing or publishing, so I began to do my research. I found and worked with a local illustrator. She told me about a local book publishing company in my area, and I contacted them. The idea would be that they would lay out the design of my book and print the book. They also had stores that I could possibly consign with.

Once the writing and illustrating process was complete — and that took several years — I contacted the publishing company. They completed the draft layout of my book, and I was able to see a sample. I liked the design, and was ready to move forward until I really gave it some more thought. In order to get the price down per book, I was going to need to order hundreds, if not thousands, of copies. I would then have all of these copies to market and sell. I realized that this was not going to be financially possible. As a new writer, I did not have thousands of dollars to invest. I could have pitched my book to a traditional publisher, however, my book was already complete: designed and formatted. I decided to go the self-publishing route.

Once the approval process was done, the book and e-book were listed for sale. They were also listed on Amazon and Barnes and Noble online. Through these platforms, CreateSpace receives a royalty percent, and they send me a percent. With self-publishing, you are responsible for all marketing. This is something important to consider when deciding to self-publish. At the time, I decided to self-publish as opposed to pitching my book to traditional publishers. Because I wrote a children's book, I've marketed my book to parents, schools, and other organizations. I also pair with local businesses to schedule book readings and signings, and partner with some bookstores to do consignment. While with self-publishing, you can make more royalties, there are also advantages to traditional publishing.

I am currently working on other book projects that are focused on women in business, and I am in the process of writing query letters and pitching my book to literary agents. When looking to work with a traditional publisher, many publishers do not accept direct manuscript submissions. Most require you to go through a literary agent. If you are selected by an agent, he or she will pitch your book to publishers. When finding a literary agent, it is important to do research: talk to other authors and research online to find literary agents that may represent the genre of your book. The second step is to evaluate the preference of the literary agent — meaning that different agents ask for different requirements — when submitting a query. Many agents currently accept emailed queries, however, some prefer mail.

I have used "Publishers Marketplace" as a resource to search for literary agents, but "Writers Market" is another resource. I have also talked to other authors for advice and suggestions, and you may be able to go to your local library for resources. I have pitched to several literary agents and have been declined. My piece of advice is that finding an agent and publisher can be challenging, but don't give up. If you try and then feel it's time to self-publish, then that's OK too.

The advantage to having a publisher is that they have the capability of getting your books into bookstores that don't necessarily accept self-published books. Also, books that are published through a publisher tend to have higher credibility. The publishing companies do get higher royalties than if you self-publish, and you are still expected to promote your book. Having the connections of a publisher, however, can be very beneficial.

There are people who you can hire to promote your book, although you can market yourself in several ways. Research book bloggers and send them your information to possibly review your book. Other ideas include participating in social media groups relating to books and literacy, social media promotion, and local book readings and signings and referrals through other authors — to name a few.

No matter which route that you decide to take when publishing, know that there are rewards and risks with both, but if you set a goal, take the steps, and stay determined, you can become a successful self-published or published author!

*Melissa Carter is owner of The Wholistic Package. The Wholistic Package (**www.wholistic** package. com) encompasses wellness books — including a children's book and contributions to So You Want to Write a Children's Book? — as well as products and services to empower women.*

Why self-publish?

Self-publishing is a viable option for writers of all levels. The reasons writers cite for self-publishing are as varied as the type of material they place in the market. Here are a few typical reasons to self-publish:

- You want to retain a bigger share of the profits from the sale of your book.

- Your book contains time-sensitive information and you want to get it to market faster than the traditional publishing route.

- You already have a big following—and a built in audience hungry to gobble up your words of wisdom (or wit).

- You like the idea of being completely in control of your book, from content to design to marketing.

- Your material is geared toward a small niche market and traditional publishers may consider the audience too small for them to make a profit.

- You have a book that you want to bring to market, but money is not your main motivation.

Of course, some writers decide to self-publish after trying the traditional route with no takers. Not wanting to face one more rejection, they decide to self-publish.

Some writers are "hybrid" authors. Hybrid authors use both traditional and self-publishing options to get their work to market. Many authors consider this option as the best of both worlds. Some authors have self-published first and then received traditional publishing deals. They often continue to use both mediums to publish. The reverse is also true. Some traditionally published writers have gone the self-publishing route, while continuing to churn out books with the big publishing houses. Authors with a large following are typically very successful with their self-publishing ventures. Why not? After all, they already have a loyal following.

Although self-publishing is a viable option, keep in mind if you self-publish:

- You are responsible for the cost of bringing your book to market. This includes any costs associated with book design, editing, marketing, and publicity.

- Some bookstores will not stock self-published books.

- Some contests and awards are not open to self-published authors.

Self-published authors ultimately land deals with traditional publishers. Wendy Tokunaga's self-published book *No Kidding* (2000) won honorable mention in the *Writer's Digest* International Self-Published Awards 2002 competition. This win gave her the confidence to seek an agent. Ultimately, she sold a manuscript, *Midori Moonlight* (2007), to St. Martin's press.

So, how do you get your self-published book on the market? You could print a bunch of copies at your local printer, or take the print-on-demand (POD) route, which is what most authors do.

First, let me explain how POD publishers work. As the name implies, when working with a POD publisher, books are printed on demand, meaning a book is only printed when a customer orders one. This is a great option for authors.

Before the popularity of POD publishing, authors had to order a bunch of books from a printer. This meant you had to pay upfront for books that you may not have been able to eventually sell. Plus, you had to store the books *and* ship them out. Not an ideal situation.

With POD publishing, the upfront costs are lower, you do not have to stock your books, and you do not have to worry about shipping out orders. *Whew!* This leaves time for more important things like writing your next book.

All POD publishers are not created equal. There are hundreds of companies to choose from, so you will have to do a bit of research to find the one that works for you. Fortunately, this guide will give you a jumpstart. The appendix lists some of these publishers, but for now, let's take a closer look at two popular, and affordable, POD options.

CreateSpace

CreateSpace is Amazon's self-publishing platform. Free, easy-to-use tools allow authors to quickly publish their books and retain a higher percentage of royalties than other print-on-demand publishers. Here's what you get with CreateSpace:

Copyright: Authors retain copyright of their work.

An interior reviewer: After uploading your book file, the reviewer will look for formatting issues. For example, you may have text or images that fall outside the margin. After alerting you to these issues, you can then go back and make changes to your document.

A cover creator: A great book deserves a great cover. You can use your own images, or select from CreateSpace's gallery, along with pre-designed templates to create a stunning cover for your work.

Distribution: You can sell your book through Amazon.com, your own e-store, and through expanded channels like bookstores, online retailers, and libraries.

ISBN: All books must have an **International Standard Book Number (ISBN)**. This unique numerical code identifies your book from the millions of other books on the market. CreateSpace offers a free ISBN. If you choose the free option, you can only publish your book through CreateSpace. You can also purchase a custom ISBN for $99.00. This option allows you to use the ISBN with any publisher. For example, if you are not satisfied with CreateSpace, you can publish with another company, using the same ISBN. The third option is to use your own ISBN, which you can purchase through Bowker, the official seller of ISBNs, or through an authorized agency.

Paid add-on services: If you want to leave the designing to the professionals, you can hire someone to create your book's cover. Need help editing? Yep, you can also hire an editor to copyedit (look for grammar, typos, etc.) or line edit (offer suggestions relating to structure and flow, in addition to grammatical issues) your work. Prices vary based on the type of service you require. For example, you'll pay $160.00 for copy editing and $210.00 for line editing for manuscripts up to 10,000 words. A custom cover design will cost $399.00.

Publishing Formats: Softcover (black & white and full color), e-books.

Royalty: Your royalty payment is calculated using this formula:

**The list price (you set your own price) – CreateSpace's share
= Your Royalty**

CreateSpace's share includes a percentage of the list price, a fixed charge, and in some cases, a per-page fee. A handy royalty calculator is available to show you exactly what you can expect to receive in royalties from each distribution channel. This way, there are no surprises: For example:

If the list price for your book—175 pages, black and white interior, 5 x 8 trim size—is: $ 9.95, you would earn the following royalties across these three channels:

Through Amazon.com	$3.01
From your own Amazon e-store	$5.00
Through Expanded Distribution	$1.02

Up-front Publishing Fees: Once your book is complete, you have the option of ordering a printed review copy or you can review electronically for free. The cost of the printed book is the fixed charge, per-page charge plus shipping and handling.

Lulu

Lulu is a popular publishing platform. Here are some of the perks of publishing with Lulu.

Copyright: Author retains copyright.

Cover & Interior Design Templates: You can download both interior and book cover templates to aid you in designing your book. All templates are easily customizable. Once you upload your completed project, Lulu will convert your files into a print ready PDF document. You can then download your book for review.

Distribution: Lulu, Amazon, Barnes & Noble, and Ingram

ISBN: Free ISBN or you can purchase your own.

Paid add-on services: You can pay for a variety of design, editing, and marketing packages. All-inclusive bundled packages currently range from $999 to $2999 for a black & white book, and $1199 to $3199 if your book is full color. You can also pay for individual services. "Elite Cover Design" will cost you $599. Need line editing? You will pay $.037 per word.

Publishing Formats: Softcover, hardcover, and e-book

Royalty: If distributed on Lulu.com, Lulu subtracts the base price (the cost to manufacture the book) and a commission from the retail price of your book to determine your share. For example, the cost of a 6x9, 100 page, black & white paperback book is $3.25. This does not include Lulu's share. Once you set up an account, you can play around with the calculator to determine exactly how much you will make on the sale of each book.

Up-front Publishing Fees: If you are doing all of the work yourself, you will only pay for the cost of a review copy(s).

Expresso Book Machine– Print Your Books Vending Machine-Style

If you are really in hurry to get your self-published book printed, you may be able to print your book from a vending machine. Yep, I said a vending machine. The Expresso Book Machine, the brain-child of On Demand Books, offers POD services, but what makes them different than other companies is that authors print their own books, in person, at one of the companies' book machines.

The service takes your print-ready PDF files and spits out a bound paperback book, with a color cover and black & white interior.

You can print from 40 to 800 pages and in a variety of trim sizes. It takes only a few minutes to produce one book. Of course, you will have to distribute your own books, but this option may work for authors who plan to sell their books directly to the public. For instance, at fairs, festivals, church and community events, etc.

Locations include many libraries and bookstores, including:

- Shakespeare & Company, an independent bookstore in New York

- University of Arizona Library

- Barnes & Noble in New York

- Brigham Young University Bookstore in Provo, Utah

- Boxcar and Caboose Bookshop, an independent bookstore in St. Johnsbury, Vermont

A word of caution about vanity presses

A vanity press is "a publishing house that publishes books at the author's expense—called also vanity publisher."[39]

A word of caution is in order. As you enter the publishing world, you need to be aware that scams exist. A classic example is the vanity press. Some people will try to fool writers by waving the small or indie press banner. But, make no mistake, a vanity press by any other name is rotten to the core.

These unscrupulous scoundrels prey on a writer's vanity. Some writers want to see their name in print so bad that they will pay for the privilege. Al-

---

39. **www.merriam-webster.com**, 2016.

An editor can also point out your manuscript's strengths as well as highlight potential errors, says Gibson. Before you hire an editor, you have to figure out which type of editor you need, Gibson adds. A developmental editor will read your manuscript and give you feedback about important elements like structure, style, and voice. If you want an editor to copyedit or proofread your manuscript, he or she will look for issues such as grammatical or spelling errors or problems with continuity.

Although all 10 of Gibson's tips are important, I believe the first one is vitally important: "You should avoid the temptation to hire someone to edit your first draft."[43]

In a rush to get your wonderful book into the hands of an adoring audience, you should not expect an editor (or even a friend, your grandma, or your writing group), to slog through a poorly written first draft. Yes, I said poorly written. No matter how gifted a writer you are, your first draft is probably going to have some stinky parts that will need to be taken out like three-day-old garbage.

Just make sure the editor you choose is legitimate and qualified. I have heard horror stories of writers getting burned by unqualified editors. These authors ended up with a poorly edited manuscript and empty pockets.

The first three chapters in this guide have equipped you with a lot of the tools you need to get started today on the road to successfully publishing your book, but there is still a lot of ground to cover. In the next chapter, we look at an alternative to print—e-books.

---

43. Gibson, 2013.

Chapter 4: *Publishing an E-book*

Despite doomsday predictions, print is not dead. However, printed books aren't the only way for authors to reach readers. New digital technologies have opened up a new way to publish — electronically.

Publishing an electronic book (e-book) is an affordable way for authors to distribute their work. An author can create an e-book in addition to a print version or as a stand-alone. This chapter guides you through the process of successfully publishing an e-book.

Why E-Publish?

We live in an age of instant gratification. We want fast food, drive-thru emergency rooms, and instant downloads. It seems only natural that e-books are the next big wave in publishing. With the click of a mouse, a reader can buy your book and start *oohing* and *aahing* over your poetic words quicker than driving to a bookstore. They can avoid the headaches of driving in heavy traffic. When they arrive, they have to look for your book, stand in a long line, then drive all the way back home. Finally, they are able to crack open your book.

Whew! I'm exhausted just thinking about it. Readers can order books on-line but then they have to wait days for them to arrive. Authors with a loyal fan base, can easily sell stand-alone e-books. They often create e-books for fans while working on the print edition of their next novel.

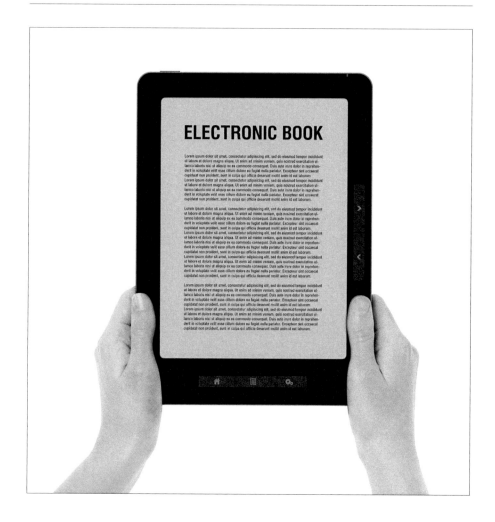

Many new authors are finding success as e-book publishers, often seeing their titles on bestseller lists alongside books from big publishing houses, according to an article in the February 2014 issue of *Writer's Digest* ("What Writers Need to Know About the E-book Market"). The author, Jeremy Greenfield, points out an important perk for self-published e-book authors: distribution of their digital work to libraries. The "Big Five" have customarily used this distribution channel and now this option is available for most self-published e-book authors.

From a publishing standpoint electronic publishing is cost-effective. If you self-publish, you may have to make an initial investment if you hire someone to edit or design your book. Otherwise, it's cheaper to publish an e-book.

The same is true if you have a traditional publisher. Once your book is published, shipping and distribution costs are *nil, nada, zilch, zero*—you get my point. There's no returns to deal with, either. Let's look at a few additional reasons why publishing an e-book is a good idea.

High profit margin: E-book authors usually receive a higher percent of the sales price from an e-book than from a print edition. If you self-publish and sell directly from your website, you can pocket 100 percent of the profits.

Longevity: Print books have a limited shelf life. After initial runs, publishers usually won't print additional copies unless the book does enormously well. E-books never go out of print, unless you or the publisher take them off the market.

It's easier to offer specials deals to potential customers: It's easy to offer free chapters to entice readers to purchase the whole book. As an avid reader, I'm more likely to purchase a book, especially by a "new to me" author, if I can sample the words first.

The low price makes e-books an ideal impulse buy: How many of you have bought something because it was on sale? I can't see how many hands went up, but I know I'm not the only one. Later in this chapter we talk about pricing e-books but for now the thing you need to know is most e-books are cheap. This makes them an ideal impulse buy. Most of us wouldn't think twice about paying $2.99 for an e-book. We probably would think twice (or thrice) about paying $24.95 for a print book. With some books selling for $.99, readers often scoop up two or more. Some authors offer books for free (we'll discuss this later also) to entice readers to purchase additional books.

No additional marketing required if you have a print book: If you're publishing a print book, the good news is you won't have to do any additional marketing to sell your e-book. Most online shoppers will automatically look for e-book versions. If you're publishing an e-book separately, you can use the same marketing strategies you would to market a print version.

E-books can enhance reader experience: E-books aren't motionless like their print cousins. As a way to improve the reader's experience, enhancements are often added such as audio or video clips. You can also add music, a photo gallery or have a narrator read the text. Some e-books offer readers the option of looking up the definition of an unfamiliar word. Other enhancements include the ability to access background information, write notes, search within text, and enlarge text.

Easy to update: One of biggest perks of creating an e-book is the ease of updating information—especially for non-fiction books. Non-fiction titles and reference e-books can always have the most up-to-date information.

Authors can experiment in ways they wouldn't be able to do with print: An author can release segments of work-in-progress and receive feedback. They can ask readers to help decide the direction of the plot. Authors can offer prequels, sequels or write short stories that focus on minor or secondary characters from previously published novels or an ongoing series. Authors can sell subscriptions or serialize their books. Basically, e-books allow authors to experiment without investing a lot of money.

> ## *BookShots*
>
> Even best-selling authors are jumping on the e-book bandwagon. James Patterson brings his Alex Cross, Michael Bennett, Women's Murder Club, and other characters to life in small doses. Book-Shots (www.bookshots.com) features original 150-page stand-alone stories. Readers can access these tiny tales on any iOS or Android device. The books currently sell for $3.99 or $9.99 for the audio version.

The cost to convert a book to e-book format is low: If your book is being traditionally published, you won't need to worry about creating an e-book edition. If you're self-publishing a print book and want to offer an e-book option, most POD services, like Amazon's CreateSpace, will easily convert your files. You can use a conversion service or purchase software that will walk you through the conversion process.

So as you can see, e-books are a great publishing option. Of course, we need to also look at the cons.

Print books last longer: I love technology, but I also love the smell of old musty books. I love going to the library or used bookstore and browsing, hoping to find an old treasure. Although e-books don't go out of print, the e-reader you're using today will probably not last more than a few years. Either the technology will change (and possibly you won't be able to access your library) or your device will go *kaput*, as devices often do. Properly stored books can last for eons.

Technological changes may make your books unreadable: Technological advances move at warp speed. Even if you take good care of your reader, there's a chance you won't be able to purchase new e-books unless you upgrade. This is because of changes in file formatting and upgrades to the readers. Companies will always respond to consumers need for bigger, faster, stronger, better devices. The reader you are enjoying today may become an expensive paperweight tomorrow.

You can't always read an e-book when you want to: Reading a print book is easy. You simply open one up and let your eyeballs scan the page. Reading an e-book is dependent on the whims of technology. If your battery is dead, you can't read your book. Most apps require an Internet connection to access special features. No connection means no special features.

You could lose your library if you misplace or damage your reader: It's easy to replace print books you lose, especially if it's only one book. If your reader is lost, stolen or your puppy confuses it for a chew toy (bad puppy!), you have lost your entire library. You may be able to access your library from the retailer, but you will need to go through the process of buying a new reader and downloading your books again.

Not all books work in e-book format: What type of book are you planning to write? Suppose you decide to write a cookbook. A cookbook is a good example of the type of book that may not work well as an e-book. It's hard to scroll through or flip the pages with one hand, while cooking with the other. Plus, you can possibly damage your reader by dropping liquids on it.

Books with lots of vibrant photographs, like art books, are probably best published in print format. Although enhancements are nice, some books for small children, such as lift the flap and pop-outs, are also best suited for print books.

E-books are designed for specific readers: You don't need any special equipment to read a print book. Except maybe a pair of glasses. However, e-book readers are not universal. A book designed for the Kindle, can't be read on the Nook and vice versa. You have to keep this in mind when creating your book. You can offer it in different formats, but you'll have to invest the time (if you self-publish) to do so. Otherwise, readers will have to use conversion software to read your book.

FAST FACT

"As of mid-January 2016, Amazon's US -book sales were running at a rate of *1,064,000 paid downloads a day.*"[44]

Identifying Your Audience

You may think the audience for e-books is the same as for print. Although there is some overlap and e-readers are relatively inexpensive, not everyone owns the technology to read an e-book. The good news is the market is still substantial and growing daily.

---

44. Authorearnings.com, 2016.

So who are your readers? According a report released by Pew Research Center [45], which covers adults over the age of 18 who had read an e-book during the previous year:

- 28 percent read an e-book in the previous 12 months

- Women are more likely to have read an e-book than men

- The highest percentage by race (30 percent) of readers was African-American

- 18-29 year olds comprised the highest percentage (37 percent) by age

- 45 percent of e-book readers were college grads

- Most readers have incomes over $75,000 (46 percent)

- The highest percentage of e-book readers (31percent) live in the suburbs

- 87 percent of e-book readers also read a print book

What type of devices are readers using? According to the report:

- 87 percent use an e-reader (Nook, Kindle, etc.)

- 78 percent use tablets

- 31 percent use computers

- 32 percent use their phone

Does this mean you should only target people that fall within the above demographics? No. As with any research project, only a sample of the pop-

---

45. Zuckuhr and Rainie. 2014.

ulation are selected to participate. But, it's a good idea to know who your potential readers could be.

E-Publishing Options

If you are self-publishing your e-book, you need to decide which publishing route you'll take. Here are the easiest routes to get your e-book into the hands of readers.

Upload directly to an online retailer

Major players like Barnes & Noble's NOOK Press and Amazon's Kindle Direct Publishing make it easy for e-book authors to publish their work along with titles from big publishing houses. Let's take a closer look at the process of publishing with these two giants.

Barnes & Noble's Nook Press

Authors can self-publish e-books through NOOK Press quickly and have their work distributed through BN.com and on NOOK devices. Your agreement with NOOK Press is not exclusive so you can sell your books through other distribution channels. The easy-to-use platform will walk you through the process of getting your manuscript ready for electronic publication.

The sign-up process is painless. Once you have an account, all the tools you need for success are a mouse click away.

There's no charge to publish your book. For each book sold, a percentage of sales goes to NOOK according to the current payment schedule. Here's the royalty rate as of January 2017:

List Price	Royalty Rate
$0.99 - $2.98	40 %
$2.99 - $9.99	65 %
$10.00 - $199.99	40 %

Let's do some math shall we? Here's a micro quiz:

If the retail price of your e-book is $9.99, how much will you make on the sale of each book?

A. $3.97

B. $6.49

C. ¯_(ツ)_/¯ I flunked math

The correct answer is. . . . '**B**'. That's $9.99 x 65 %. If you got the correct answer, you're a regular smarty pants. If you answered 'C', consider getting a tutor.

E-books created through NOOK Press are readable on the NOOK e-reader or users can download free software that will work on non-NOOK devices including Android and iOS devices, Macs, and PCs.

After you complete a project, the turn-around time is 24-72 hours before your book is available for purchase. If you need to replace your book—no biggie—simple upload the edited version and easily replace the old manuscript. You'll need to upload a cover image to display on the product page.

Hopefully, you have properly formatted and designed your manuscript before you upload to NOOK. If not, the manuscript editor will make sure your book meets NOOK's formatting requirements. You can also type your manuscript directly into the editor. If you want to see what your book will look like, you can preview it or download it as an EPUB file, once your book goes on sale. EPUB is short for electronic publishing. Files have the extension ". epub" and are readable on any device.

Amazon's Kindle Direct Publishing

If you self-publish a print book through Amazon's CreateSpace, you can easily turn your manuscript into an e-book. Or you can create a stand-alone e-book via Kindle Direct Publishing (KDP), Amazon's e-book publishing imprint. After creating an account (or signing in with an existing Amazon account), you can publish an e-book quickly and have it available for purchase within 24-48 hours.

Your books are sold in the Amazon Kindle store and readable on Kindle devices or apps. Once you upload your manuscript, KDP will automatically convert your book for the Kindle. You can read through the formatting guidelines to make sure the process runs smoothly once you upload your manuscript. If all goes well, you can complete the entire process in less than 30 minutes.

Through an independent e-book distributor

Barnes & Noble and Amazon aren't the only two players in the e-book game. Authors can publish and distribute their work using Smashwords, which claims to be the largest distributor of independent e-books.

E-publishing with Smashwords

Unlike other self-publishing services, Smashwords only publishes e-books. So you can assume they spend a lot of time perfecting their business model. Here are a few of the bonuses when you publish using their platform:

High royalties: Authors earn a 60 percent royalty from their books when sold through Smashwords' retail partners and up to 80 percent when sold directly from the platforms' website.

Largest distribution network: You can sell your books to a large network of retailers and libraries including Barnes & Noble, iBooks, Scribd., Over-Drive, and Baker & Taylor. Your agreement with Smashwords is non-exclusive though, which means you can choose to sell your book wherever you want – even if you only use their service to convert your manuscript.

No fee to publish: The platform is free to use. Any upfront fees are ones you incur if you hire someone to edit, format or design your book. Smashwords does not offer any publishing packages.

Ease of distribution: Smashwords takes the hassle out of distributing your book to multiple retailers. All you have to do is upload your manuscript once. After your book is published, Smashwords will distribute it to multiple retailers and libraries. Your book is available almost immediately in the Smashwords store.

Easy to use publishing platform: Smashwords offers a simple step-by-step user interface. They also offer free ISBNs and easy file conversion. Plus, you have access to free marketing and sales tools. If you need to make changes, for example you offer a discount on your book, just make the changes from your dashboard and all of the retailers will automatically receive updates.

No worries about devices: Most of the books can be read on any device. When a customer purchases your book, they select the type of device they own.

Fast fact: Not sure how to price your book? Smashwords allows authors to choose a ***Reader-Sets-the-Price*** option (R.S.P.). Readers can pay whatever they want for your book, if you choose this option. This option is not available through the retail channels though, only through the Smashwords store.

Offers pre-orders: You can start selling your book before it's officially published. Smashwords offers a pre-order option through a few of their retail partners. As of January 2017, Apple iBooks, Barnes & Noble and Kobo, accept pre-orders. Customers can place orders in advance of the release date but the retailer won't charge their credit card until the book is released.

Author interviews: Readers can find out more about authors by reading a Q& A (question and answer) interview, accessible by clicking on the author's name.

How to publish on Smashwords in 3 easy steps

Publishing on Smashwords is quick and easy. Just follow these directions:

1. Open an account.

2. Use the handy style guide to properly format your manuscript using Microsoft Word.

3. Upload and publish.

See, I told you it was easy.

Sell directly from your website

You can cut out the middle man and keep most (or all) of your profits by selling directly from your website. There are two ways to do this. You can use a conversion service if you want to make your book available on different types of e-readers. You can use a free service (like Smashwords) or pay to have your manuscript properly converted.

A second option is to create your book in PDF format. This costs nothing, and the book can be read by anyone with a program that reads these types of files. You can easily convert your Microsoft Word documents to PDF format with a click of a button. Don't have Word? No worries, if you are using Google Docs, you can also download your files in PDF format.

If you want to test the waters without spending a lot of money, a PDF book may be a practical solution to your publishing needs.

Do You Need an ISBN number?

If you have a print version of your book, you may think you can slap the same number on your e-book. Not so fast cousin. The ISBN number for a print book is unique to that edition and can't be used for an electronic version.

Since e-books aren't shipped, technically an ISBN number is not required. However, it's a good idea to get one anyway. Most publishers will give you a free ISBN number or you can purchase one on the cheap. Some retailers won't stock your e-book without an ISBN number. To list your e-book in most catalogs and directories, an ISBN number is required. If you plan to sell only through your personal website, then you can skip this step. But with the ease of acquiring a number, it might be worth it to go ahead and get one.

E-Readers

As mentioned most e-books published for one platform won't be accessible on a different one. But things are changing. With services like Smashwords and other conversion apps and services, hopefully one day your reader's e-reader will not matter.

So things are looking up for authors concerned that their book won't be accessible to all potential readers no matter their device preference. When planning your book, you can decide to publish on your preferred e-reader or leave it up to customers to find a way to open your book. Maybe one day there will be a universally accepted e-book format readable on all e-readers. But for now, the popular readers, along with books created in PDF and EPUB formats are the main ways readers will access your books.

Formatting

If you're self-publishing an e-book you should have a basic understanding of how to format the manuscript for easy conversion. One thing to keep in mind is unlike a print book, you won't have any control over the way your e-book displays on the screen.

The text that appears on the screen is *reflowable*, meaning it adapts to fit the size of the screen. The appearance may also differ because the user changes the font size or style. Ditto for page numbers, don't spend too much time worrying about these particular characteristics.

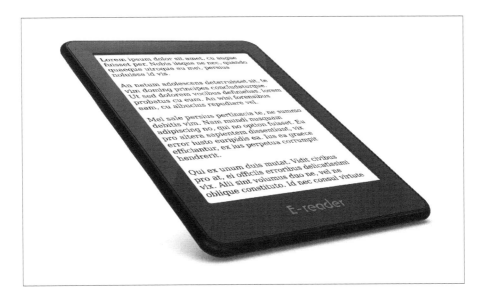

Don't get me wrong, you still want to make sure your book is pleasing to the eye, but some of the pretty formatting you spend hours worrying about may not look the same after your book is converted or by the time it reaches your reader's eyes.

When you decide where you want to publish your e-book, you can check the style guide to make sure you prepare your manuscript for easy conversion. The guides are specific to each platform, however, here are a few tips to keep in mind when preparing your manuscript.

Creating content for e-readers

K.I.S.S. (Keep It Short Sweetie) your paragraphs: A reader staring at a large block of text may get discouraged. Instead, write in short paragraphs – three to five sentences work well.

Use lists when possible: Readers love lists. When possible, present information in list format instead of large chunks of text.

Use chapters and sub-chapters: An easy way for readers to navigate through your book is to divide it into chapters and sub-chapters. Grouping your information into segments that convey the same concept is also a way to help readers quickly find the information they need.

Send images as separate files: It's okay to use images in your manuscript but most services require you to send the images in a separate compressed file. Check the guidelines for specifics on how to compress and send your image files.

Some characters won't look the same on e-readers: If you use special characters or glyphs, they may not look the same when converted. A glyph is "a hieroglyphic character or symbol." [46] In other words, think pictograph. The symbol may look snazzy in a Microsoft Word document but look like trash on a Kindle.

Book Copy Can Make a Sale or Brand You as an Amateur

If you're self-publishing, you need to create book copy to sell your book. This goes for both print and electronic version. Since e-books are often impulse buys, it is doubly important to make sure your book copy sparkles.

What do I mean by book copy? I'm not speaking about the content of your book but the short paragraph that explains what your book is about. How well you're able to hook the reader will determine if they hit "purchase" or move on to the next book. I don't care how beautifully designed your book cover is, if your book copy is lacking you could lose sales. Recently, I saw a beautifully designed e-book, but I was unable to get past the mix up of "they're" and "their" in the book copy. Maybe it was a simple typo. I don't know. But the writer lost me as a potential buyer.

You need a strong headline that will hook the reader like a fish flopping around in the sea waiting for someone to reel him in. You want to give the reader just enough information to know what the book is about and why they should read it. The "what's in it for me" angle.

Don't rush through this process. Otherwise, no one will read the contents of your awesome book.

---

46. En.Oxforddictionaries.com, 2017.

Protection from Copyright Infringement and Electronic Theft

A major concern for many e-book authors is the thief of their creative work. It is easier for thieves to steal an electronic document and slap their name on it than a print version they have to physically sit down and re-type.

Protection from copyright infringement is an issue worth discussing. Not to scare or dissuade you from publishing an e-book, but to make sure you are aware that it could happen. What do I mean by copyright infringement? We have already discussed copyright. Normally, you as the author, will hold the copyright for work you create (unless you have sold all rights to the publisher). Infringement is a violation of a law, so copyright infringement is fancy way of saying someone knowingly stole your work and passed it off as their own.

A thief may try to steal your book for two reasons:

1. To pass the work off as their own

2. Because they are too cheap to buy it

Either way, you have to accept that if you put content in electronic format, someone may steal it.

Digital Rights Management (DRM) software

If there's any good news about the potential theft of your work, it's this: most thieves don't want your book for copyright infringement; they want to read it without paying for it. I know that's not necessarily a good thing because they are literally taking money out of your pocket. But it's better than taking your work, slapping their name on it and passing it off as their own *and* making money from it.

Fortunately, distributors of e-books use software to control who has access to your e-books. A book with *Digital Rights Management* (DRM) software can only be opened and read *after* a customer pays for it. Other protection includes:

- Preventing a book from being printed or copied

- Limiting how many times a customer can download a copy of the book

- Linking it to a particular e-reading device (to prevent sharing)

- Not allowing screenshots

Free books, of course, don't need the added protection of DRM because well, they're free for everyone to download. DRM software uses encryption that makes the files look like a bunch of gobbledygook:

*ZZZZ IMSTB BWTGL VUPUF PQFOH LIUPP IAXND UCPGS
XCKBC IFDNT DULWJ*

*BBVVA NLCNV KJQVW HKBFJ SLROT QCWWP MDMLP NWJEP
WTJHX RAWJM*

Unless the thief has way too much time on his or her hands to try and figure out the encryption key—and let's face it, thieves are typically lazy bums—the pilfered book won't be readable. Boom! In your face, crook.

FAST FACT

Encrypting a file solves the problem of an illegally-gained copy not being readable. But once the file is decrypted, there's nothing to stop someone from passing their copy around to others.

If you are self-publishing your e-book and selling it directly from your own website without using any type of service — if your book is a PDF file — you can take steps to make sure your work is not used nefariously (for evil or wicked purposes). You can still use DRM software or some of the built in document protection that will prevent your book from being copied.

Types of DRM software

In the same way as an e-book created for one type of electronic device can't be opened and read on another device (unless you are using a special app), an e-book protected with one type of DRM software cannot be accessed by a different type of DRM software. Each e-book distributor uses a different type of DRM, for example:

- Apple's iBooks uses FairPlay

- Kindle uses a proprietary DRM

- Adobe Content Server is used for ePub and PDF files

You (or your publisher) will have to make the decision whether to DRM-protect your book prior to publication. You can't let a puppy out of an open gate, *then* lock it and expect him not to run away. Once you release your puppy (your book) without DRM protection, you can't tell readers what to do with it. You can un-publish it and add the protection, but at this point unprotected copies are floating around.

Some authors forgo DRM because they figure the potential for future book sales is greater than the cost and hassle of protecting their work. If you're publishing traditionally, you may not have a say so in this issue, but as a self-published author it's your decision.

Keep in mind, tech-savvy hackers can always find their way around most types of DRM protection anyway. If you are concerned that someone may sell copies of your book (either under their name or unauthorized selling under your name), there are legal steps you can take if this happens.

Pricing Your E-book

Now we arrive at the important issue of how to price your book. There's no set formula you can plug in to help you decide. Here are some tips to keep in mind though:

A lower price usually translates into bigger sales. As mentioned earlier, for some readers e-books are impulse buys. Sort of like the reason I have four sets of holes in my ears. I got my ears pierced for the first time when I was eighteen. Years later, I got a second set. Fast forward a few years later and on a dare, I got a third set. Since I was already in the hot seat, I impulsively got a fourth set. *Ahhh* the impulsivity of my youthful years. Where was I? Oh, impulse buys, right. Okay, so a reader is more likely to buy your book if the price is right. Even if they ultimately hate it, they won't feel so bad that they plunked down a buck fifty to read your drivel. If they spent $9.99 or more, you can probably expect them to trash your book on Amazon.

Start low; adjust if necessary. You can play around with different pricing strategies until you find a price that works for you. It's best to start with a low price and adjust upwards, rather than a higher price, then slash it -- although you could use this strategy to trick customers into thinking they are getting a deal. Who doesn't like a deal? No one. Another option is to offer a time-limited low price. This sense of urgency will prompt readers sitting on the fence to actually get off the fence, grab their wallet, and tap in their credit card information.

Entice readers with samples. You could offer free excerpts to encourage readers to buy the whole book, or you can sell a low-priced excerpt. Most people would be willing to pay a few dollars to sample a book with an interesting plot. Here's where writing great book copy comes in handy.

Keep readers wanting more by serializing your work. A potentially profitable way to make more money from your work is to serialize it. When you serialize a book, you sell it to readers (or subscribers) a small chunk at a time. The key is to present information that leaves readers wanting more. For a novel, it should be a real page turner. Readers should be so hungry for what happens next that they will gladly pay for the next installment.

Serialized e-books can span any genre. Non-fiction titles work just as well as novels or memoirs. The trick is to leave readers craving more. There is flexibility if you decide to serialize your work. You can complete the entire manuscript before offering it for sale, or write it as you go. If you choose the latter, you have to create a publishing schedule and stick to it. You definitely don't want to anger readers by promising the next installment on a particular date and have them waiting for you to finish.

Wattpad

If you want to try your hand at publishing but want to get feedback from readers as you write, then you may want to try publishing your book on the Wattpad (www.wattpad.com) platform.

Once you open an account, you can start creating your book directly from within your dashboard or import your manuscript.

When your book is ready, just click publish, and send it out into the world. You post your books one chapter at a time and readers can make comments along the way. This is a great opportunity for writers to see what works and doesn't work for readers. Based on their feedback, you can change your manuscript (or take it with a grain of salt). You won't make any money–the books are offered to readers for free–but if you're looking for feedback, Wattpad readers' responses may help you polish your manuscript before you send it off to an agent or publisher. Of course, you can also take the finished product and self-publish through one of the platforms mentioned in this chapter.

Offer free books. What kind of lame pricing strategy is this? As with other offers, you are looking to create a loyal fan base. You can start by offering one of your books for free. Even, if you add restrictions—free to the first 50 customers or to your social media followers through a special link, for example.

Publishing your book in electronic format can be an inexpensive and quick entry into the publishing world. If you want to dip your toe in the water without jumping in head first, you should definitely consider this option. In the next chapter, we take a look at literary agents, how they can help get you published—and help you decide if you really need one.

Chapter 5: *Literary Agents*

You have a great story to tell; now you need someone to help sell your idea to a publisher. This person is called a literary agent. This chapter covers all the basics you need to know about literary agents, and will help you decide if you need one.

What Does a Literary Agent Do?

A literary agent is not your fairy godmother (or godfather). Don't expect to have all your wishes granted with a wave of a magic wand. Agents work on commission—meaning they only get paid when they land a publishing deal for their clients.

Agents must understand the publishing world. They stay on top of trends and monitor which editors are coming and going. They know when new publishing houses open and when old ones close. They cultivate relationships with editors and other professionals in the publishing world. In other words, they do a lot of the legwork so you can concentrate on writing.

Agents help new (and not so new) writers navigate the often-confusing world of publishing. Think of an agent as your representative, a middleman between you and the publisher. An agent's job is to sell your manuscript or book proposal to a publisher. Your agent should also work to negotiate the best deal for you. Agents have an interest in seeing their clients succeed. The more money an author makes, the higher an agent's commission.

Let's take a look at some of the responsibilities of a literary agent:

- Reviews query letters, manuscripts, and proposals from writers seeking representation

- Offers suggestions on edits and rewrites

- Submits manuscripts and proposals to editors and publishers; follows up on submissions

- Explains contract details to authors after an offer is received from a publisher

Do I Need a Literary Agent?

This is a question on the mind of most writers. If you self-publish, the short answer is "no". If your goal is to place your manuscript with one of the "Big Five", an agent is a must. Many smaller publishers accept nonagented material. It's possible to get a publishing deal without having an agent, however, having an agent comes with many benefits.

- **Agents know which editors would be interested in acquiring your work.** Agents spend a lot of time schmoozing with editors. They may take them out to lunch or for coffee. As they nurture these relationships, agents learn what type of material editors are currently looking to publish. This insider information helps agents submit your work to the appropriate publisher.

- **Editors prefer agent submission**. Editors are busy people and don't have a lot of time to read submissions that may not be ready for publication, not to mention the knuckleheads who submit work to a publisher that does not publish the genre submitted. Working with an agent means the manuscript has already been screened and has publishing potential. Submission from an agent means your manuscript will get read quicker. Although a smaller publisher may accept nonagented manuscripts or proposals, the response time is usually longer.

- **An agent can get you a better deal.** Agents will work hard to get you the best possible deal. If more than one publisher is interested in your manuscript, an agent can set off a bidding war. Unless you are good at negotiating, you may want to go with an agent.

- **Contracts 101.** Agents are familiar with all of the legal ramblings found in a contract. An agent's job is to make sure the details in the contract benefit the author. An agent's job is also to explain the details of the contract and help you weigh your options. Without an agent, an author has very little wiggle room to negotiate a better deal.

- **An agent gives you more time for important stuff—like writing.** Your agent will handle mundane issues that would keep you from having more time to write. Your agent will deal with rejection letters and track payments. They will handle publicity, marketing, and legal issues, also.

- **Sometimes it *is* who you know.** Agents cultivate relationships with editors but they also have a network of other individuals who can help you. An agent may be able get an endorsement, speaking engagement or media appearance, deals you probably couldn't land on your own.

- **Agents advocate on your behalf.** Without an agent, your book may not get as much attention from an editor or publisher. Agents will often speak on your behalf, requesting a higher marketing budget, for example. Without an agent, if your editor leaves, your project may stall.

Situations When You Probably Won't Need an Agent

There are several scenarios where you don't need an agent. In *Essential Guide to Getting Your Book Published,* authors Arielle Eckstut and David Henry Sterry examine a few of these cases. If your audience is very limited, you are a poet, or your book has regional appeal, you won't need an agent. In these cases, you are better off self-publishing or sending directly to a small or university press.

You won't need an agent if you have items that need to be packaged with your book. These items include DVDs, pens, spy rings, etc. Even a book with lots of photographs and illustrations can be a hassle for agents. The authors say these types of books usually require multiple contributors or additional problems that are best suited for a book packager. A book packager handles all of the elements needed to bring your book to market and then sells it to a traditional publisher.

Am I Ready for an Agent?

You have decided to get an agent. Congrats! Wait, not so fast. Before you start sending out queries, you need to make sure they don't boomerang back to you. The best way to cut down on your rejections is to make sure you are ready for an agent. Take this short quiz to see if you are agent-ready.

- **Do you have a publishing plan?** Remember, if you plan to self-publish, or submit to a small or academic press, you won't need an agent. For instance, poetry and short story collections are best sent to literary houses or a small press.

- **Have you done your homework?** You probably thought writing a book wouldn't involve so much homework. You need to research appropriate potential agents. You need to make sure you are targeting the right agents. If you're writing romance and send your query to an agent who does not handle romance, you can guess what's going to happen.

- **Have you created a perfectly polished pitch package?** That's a tongue twister! But if you are serious about selling your manuscript or book idea, you need to create a pitch package to send to potential agents or editors. If you're a fiction writer, a pitch package should contain a query letter, a synopsis of your book, and the completed manuscript. For non-fiction letters, send a query letter, a book proposal, and a few sample chapters. All of the material you send should sparkle like the sun on a bald man's head. If you're a fiction writer, please finish your manuscript before querying agents and editors. It may be tempting to write only the sample chapters, thinking you'll have time to complete the manuscript after you get an agent or editor, but you should be to submit your full manuscript upon request.

- **Is your manuscript idea salable?** You will have to do more homework, sorry (not sorry!). Just because you *think* your idea is wonderful does not mean it's actually a marketable idea. You have to conduct research to find out if, for example, your idea mimics books that are already on the market. Other issues to consider include the potential audience for your book, and whether the book can be serialized.

- **Do you have a promotion plan?** Many writers assume their publisher will work hard to promote their book, while they sit back and wait for the next book signing or media appearance. In the real world, authors should have their own promotion plan. This will help increase the chances an agent — and ultimately a publisher — will buy your work.

- **Have you established your platform?** Publishers are in the business of making money. It's easier for someone with a huge fan base or loyal following to get a publishing deal. That's why celebrities land six-figure deals. Although you don't need to have a bazillion followers, you should at least have some type of platform. This includes a website and social media accounts. Although it's okay to share personal information, don't use your platforms to only post pics of your cat, or Facebook Live yourself scrambling your morning eggs. Establish a professional writing platform. Chapter 7 covers this topic, so stay tuned.

- **What are your writing career goals?** Maybe you have a great idea for a book, but you don't want to make a career from writing. You want to publish one book and gracefully bow out. That's cool. However, most agents aren't looking for one-hit wonders. They prefer to work with career writers -- writers who are in it for the long haul. Don't waste an agent's time if you know you want to publish one book. If that's your objective, try self-publishing, a small press or look for a publisher accepting unagented material. At the very least be upfront with the agent.

As you can see, there's no answer key for this quiz. That's because it's more of a reflection on your goals rather than right or wrong answers. I hope you took the time to consider these important questions. If not go back and do it now. If you have areas you need to work on, please do so before stalking agents. Now, let's talk about how to land an agent once you have decided you need one.

How to Land a Literary Agent

Landing an agent may seem like the luck of the draw at times. Agents are busy and sometimes simply can't take on new clients. It's nothing personal. When evaluating your work, agents have their own criteria, but many look for certain factors. Let's take a look at some of the more important and universal ones:

The quality of your writing: Agents are looking for same things reader's want when they crack open a book: well-written, engaging copy. They look for a distinctive voice. Are you trying to write like Stephen King, Stephenie Meyer or Veronica Roth? Stop it right now and find your own voice.

Agents also want unique story lines. You don't want to bore them with yet another dystopian or vampire story do you? No. Unless you can come up with a unique spin on these tired plots, try to find an idea that has not been beaten to death. Your characters should be interesting if you're writing a novel. For non-fiction, you must choose a topic readers are interested in learning more about.

Before an agent even considers reading the full manuscript or sample chapters, your query and supplemental material (synopsis, etc.) must be compelling enough to make the agent intrigued enough to move forward.

It's all about marketing baby: When you did your homework, you identified the potential market reach of your book. In your pitch package, you need to assure the agent that your book has marketing potential. If you're pitching a book that deals with a subject already saturating the market, an agent is likely to pass, unless you have a unique perspective or angle.

The potential for subsidiary rights: Have you recently watched a movie or TV program based on a book? I'm guessing you have, even if you don't realize it. When negotiating contracts, the issue of subsidiary rights often pop up. A subsidiary right is the right ". . . to publish or produce in different formats works based on the original work under contract . . .".[47]

When evaluating your idea an agent will think of potential subsidiary rights. In addition to movies and TV, these rights might include serialization, foreign, and translations rights.

---

47. Dictionary.com, 2017.

Your author platform: Author platform: there's that phrase again. You'll hear it again in chapter 7, but for now, I want to reiterate that it's important to start working on your platform before you approach an agent. You need to establish a professional web presence.

Your potential writing career: As mentioned previously, most agents prefer career writers. They don't want to invest a lot of time and effort into placing your manuscript, then have you disappear and never write another book again.

Where Do I find a Literary Agent?

Once you make the decision to work with an agent, the hard work begins. Luckily, this guide will point you in the direction of typical avenues writers use to find their ideal agent. Here are a few of these ways:

Word-of-Mouth A.K.A Referrals: One way to find an agent is to ask other writers to recommend one. As a new writer, you may not know any writers but that's okay. If you participate in a writing workshop or group, other participants may be able to recommend an agent. You can also ask for recommendations from your virtual friends or an online writing community.

Attend Writers Conferences and Literary Events: If you live in a city that routinely or periodically hosts writing events—conference, seminars, retreats, book festivals, workshops, etc.—you may have a chance to meet an agent in person. At these events, writers can often schedule a time to meet one-on-one with an agent. These meetings are tight so you need to have a concise pitch ready to present to the agent. You can find out if a pitch session is available at the organizer's website. If you get the chance to pitch to an agent at an event, just make sure you follow up if the agent expresses an interest in seeing a query, manuscript or proposal.

FAST FACT

It's not only agents you can pitch at writing events. Sometimes editors offer pitch sessions. This is an opportunity for writers to pitch directly to a publisher without needing an agent.

Directories: Most writers turn to annual directories when looking for a literary agent. In addition to the comprehensive listing, the directories have informative articles on publishing. You can purchase these directories or check your local library to see if they have copies. The detailed guides list useful information about each agent including the types of writing he or she represents and submission guidelines. Depending on the guide, you may be able to find out other important information like the percentage of commission the agent expects and recent sales. The most widely-used directories are:

The Guide to Literary Agents published annually by Writer's Digest Books. Each guide lists hundreds of agents, plus articles on writing and publishing. You should also go online and check out the accompanying blog (http://www.writersdigest.com/editor-blogs/guide-to-literary-agents) for useful articles, agent spotlights, and more.

Jeff Herman's *Writer's Guide to Book Editors, Publishers, and Literary Agents,* is another popular and trusted source for finding an agent. Be sure to check Herman's site (http://www.jeffherman.com/) for useful publishing information. Herman is also an editor, so you can submit your non-fiction proposals to him.

The Literary Market Place is probably the most comprehensive directory available for authors seeking representation. That's the good news. The bad news is this book is outside the price range for most struggling writers. The 2017 guide costs $399.50. Luckily, most libraries carry the guide, so you can peek at a copy if one is available. You will probably have to do your snooping at the library because many guide are shelved as reference books and can't be checked out. You can also access some parts of the guide online (literarymarket-place.com) or pay for a one-week online subscription (currently $24.95).

The Internet: Most libraries carry the above popular guides. If you don't want to purchase a directory or your local library does not carry them, no worries. All you need is Internet access. You can perform a simple or advanced Internet search to get started. A better use of your time would be checking out many useful resources, like the ones below.

- **Publishers Marketplace (www.publishersmarketplace.com)**: Find out what's happening in the publishing world and look for agents on this popular site. The basic free membership works for most writers or you can pay $25 a month for paid membership. Paid members have access to additional features including information on publishing deals, a web page, and access to members-only information.

- **Publishers Weekly (www.publishersweekly.com)**: This is the go-to source for many in the publishing industry. You can find informative articles, search for an agent, or sign up for free newsletters. Publisher's Weekly recently added a section for self-published authors called, *BookLife,* which is a great addition to this already useful resource.

- **Writer's Market (www.writersmarket.com)**: You can pick up a print copy of the Writer's Market annual guide or borrow one from your library or you can subscribe to the online version for continuously updated information. If you purchase the deluxe print edition of the guide, you'll automatically get access to the online database for one year. Subscriptions as of this writing are: $5.99 monthly; $24.99 for six months, and; $39.99 for one year. Online membership includes articles, daily news updates, and an e-mail newsletter.

- **Agent Query (www.agentquery.com)**: This site hosts a free, searchable database of agents, publishing information, and networking opportunities.

- **Query Tracker (www.querytracker.net)**: This site offers a free database of agents, and a system that allows authors to keep track of their queries. The information submitted by authors is gathered into a database where other users can access information on agents like response time, the number of queries received. You can also find out how many queries are accepted or rejected by each agent.

Stalk them on Social Media: You can find agents through social media channels, like LinkedIn, Facebook, and Twitter. These avenues typically provide more up-to-date information, than found in directories and websites. Use the "search" function on any of these sites to find agents.

Identify the Literary Agent of a Book: When looking for a potential publisher, writers often look at books similar to the type they are proposing. You can do the same to find an agent. If you have a book that feels similar to the idea you're pitching, check the book to see if you can find the agent. One way is to check the dedication page, where authors often thank their agents. You can also check the author's website to see if the agent is mentioned. Search engines are also good at spitting out useful information. You can often find the agent by typing the authors name and "literary agent" in a search box.

How to Decide if an Agent is Right for You

In your eagerness to snag an agent, remember while the agent is evaluating you, you also should evaluate him or her. Don't sign with an agent just to increase your writer street cred by announcing: "I have an agent!"

There are literally thousands of agents. Before you decide which agent to pitch to, you should do your — here comes that word again — homework. You don't want to get stuck with an agent whose promises fall flat as soon as you sign on the dotted line.

Agents bring different skills and experiences to the table. Here are some areas to consider when evaluating potential agents.

Experience: Do you want to go with a new agent or an agent with more established connections in the publishing world? New agents may not have a lot of connections but you'll probably get more attention than an established agent with a large client roster.

Size of agency: Literary agencies vary in size, just like publishing houses. Most agencies are small, with only a few agents (or only one). There are also mid-sized and large agencies consisting of a handful or dozens of agents. A smaller agency will probably welcome new writers with open arms, while a larger agency may only deal with established or high profile authors.

What genre does the agent represent? Agents often represent either fiction or nonfiction writers. Some may represent both. When evaluating agents, make sure they represent your genre. Don't think your work is so great it will cause an agent to accept your work. Remember, agents cultivate relationships with certain types of editors and publishers. Although they may want to place your work, if they don't have industry contacts, they'll have a harder time, and they might pass.

What's the deal, son? Unless the agent is brand new and you are the first client, he or she should have a track record of selling books. You may still decide to go with a new agent but if an agent has been in business for a while and has only sold a handful of books, you may want to cross him or her off your list. You also want to look at recent sales. An agent who has sold 200 books but only 10 of those books have been sold in the past few years, is a cause for concern.

Association of Authors' Representatives (AAR)

Although not required, many agents belong to the Association of Authors' Representatives (http://www.aaronline.org/), a professional trade organization. Should you look for an agent with AAR-affiliation?

The biggest benefit of choosing an agent who is a member of the AAR is the agent has vowed to abide by a strict code of conduct. In other words, you probably won't get scammed by an AAR agent. As of this writing, the organization has a roster of over 400 agents. The site maintains a database of these agents and writers are welcomed to browse through when looking for representation.

The Canon of Ethics is the bible agents agree to live by, including a lot of stuff a rationale person should already know. For instance, not mixing a client's money with your own money (keeping separate bank accounts). The canon also warns agents against seeking any type of monetary compensation from clients.

Ask for References: Don't take the agent's word on how great and wonderful he or she is; ask for references from clients. An agent with nothing to hide will be happy to provide you with contact information. Or better, try cold calling (or emailing) a few clients. Explain that you are considering the agent and would like to get the skinny on him or her. This way the agent can't hand-pick who he or she wants you to talk to.

Location, Location, Location: Does it matter where your agent lives? Should you look for a New York agent? While it's not necessary to have a New York agent, it certainly won't hurt your chances of getting a publishing deal. A New York agent can better connect with editors and publishers. All of the "Big Five" are located in New York, as are many publishers of all sizes.

It's all about the Benjamins, baby: Yep, it all boils down to the moola. When evaluating an agent, find out the typical advance he or she normally gets for clients. The amount of an advance for a first-time author varies. An advance for a first-time writer from a major publishing house could range from $10,000 to $20,000. For a smaller publisher, you can expect less. If the agent you are considering acquires advances that are less than the typical rate, he or she may lack experience or negotiating skills.

Who are the authors the agent represents? : You may not recognize all of the names on the agent's client roster, but you should recognize at least a few, especially if the agent is established. Check the authors out and see what type of deals they are getting. When you look at the agent's clients, you can also see if the books he or she represent fall in your genre.

Is the agent receptive to new clients and new writers?: An established agent with a healthy client roster may not need new clients. Their plate is already full. New agents are more receptive to first-time writers. Agents also usually list on their website and in their social media circles if they are actively seeking new clients.

Does the agent charge a fee? Scams are everywhere and the publishing world is no exception. If an agent charges any type of fee, you should run, don't walk, to the nearest exit. This includes reading fees or any phrase with the word fee in it. Ditto for "retainer". If an agent asks for money upfront, it's probably a scam. Fees are different than expenses. An agent may charge you for certain fees but this information should be clearly stated in the contract.

What can you do for me? Let's say an agent is interested in representing you. You have evaluated the agent based on the information presented above. You feel this relationship could be a good fit. Should you go ahead and sign a contract? Not so fast. There's still one thing you should get clear before deciding to sign with an agent. You want specifics of how the agent will sell your book. A new agent who is trying to build a client base may be just as eager to sign up a new writer. But vague plans (or no plans) won't get your book idea sold. The agent should have at least a general idea of which editors/publishers might buy your work.

Should you set your sights on a new agent?

Eager to find representation, some authors look for new agents to help place their manuscript. Is this a good idea? There are some pros and cons of working with a new agent. In the 2017 *Children's & Illustrator's Market*, Chuck Sambuchino and Hannah Haney discuss this important topic ("New Agent Spotlights: Learn About New Reps Seeking Clients").

Some of the cons of working with a new agent include having less experience in handling contract negotiations. They may not know as many editors or have the industry connections a more experienced agent has. Longevity is also an issue. A hopeful agent may not last long if he or she is unable to get enough clients to make their business a success.

On the flip side, new agents need clients so they actively seek new writers. In the same way that a small press can offer more time with a writer, a new agent may be able to give you more attention than an agent juggling 40 or 50 clients.

The bottom line when looking for an agent–new or otherwise–is to make sure the agent has your best interests in mind.

I Have an Agent, Now What?

The hard work is behind you. Your manuscript is complete. You researched agents and found a few you think are a perfect fit. You sent out a query and one of the agents took the bait. You sent a pitch package (more about queries and pitch packages in chapter 6) and waited anxiously for a response. Finally, the agent calls with good news: "I'd like to represent you."

Great, you think. While getting a 'yes' from an agent *is* good news, there's still one important area to consider: the contract. Before you sign on the dotted line or send an electronic signature, make sure you receive a contract from your agent that clearly defines your business relationship. Here are three areas that should be clearly stated in the contract:

The agent's commission: Agents typically receive 15 percent commission on the sale of your manuscript. If an agent asks for more, ask why. The commission for foreign sales and other rights may vary. You should make sure the terms are clear. Do not assume anything.

Expenses: Although you should never pay an agent to represent you, there may be additional expenses billed to you. For example, copying or postage. With most business being conducted today electronically, you shouldn't expect to have many expenses. All expenses should be written in the contract so you're not hit with an unexpected bill. Also, put a cap on how much you are willing to pay. And ask for receipts.

Termination: Don't lock yourself into a long-term commitment. Hopefully your relationship with your new agent will work out, but it's basically a crap shoot; sometimes you win, sometimes you lose. Look for a clause that states you or the agent can terminate the agreement at any time, as long as written notice is given. The agent should receive any commissions that may occur from the sale of your manuscript prior to getting the old heave ho. Be suspicious of contracts that lock you into future work. In other words, an agent may ask you to sign a contract that covers the manuscript in question plus all future work.

Aside from the written contract, before you sign with an agent make sure you have a thorough understanding of what you can expect from the relationship. How often will the agent touch base with you? What's the agent's preferred method of contact? Make sure you know the answer to these and any other lingering questions before you sign.

The contract should be easy to understand and not filled with a lot of legal mumbo jumbo. If something is not clear, ask for clarification. If you don't like a specific term(s), it's okay to negotiate. The bottom line is you want to be perfectly happy with your choice before you trust your writing career to a stranger.

Simultaneous Submissions

Should you query more than one agent at a time? The practice of sending multiple queries at the same time is known as simultaneous submissions. It is expected and accepted that most authors will use this method when querying agents. Because the process of getting a response from an agent takes a long time, writers can't afford to wait for one agent to reply, only to receive a rejection, before moving on to the next agent. The process of responding to your query letter, manuscript, and proposals takes months. It could take years to find an agent if you are receiving rejections one at a time. If you query multiple agents, you can probably land an agent quickly.

After you have settled on a list of agents to query, the next step is to put together the perfect materials needed to convince an agent to represent you. In the next chapter, we look at these materials before ending this guide with important information you need to create your author platform. Ready? Okay, then let's turn the page.

Chapter 6: *Putting Together Your Pitch Package*

We're getting close to end of our journey, but before we say good-bye, let's look at the important issue of presenting your work to an agent or editor. When looking for an agent, you need to present your work in the best light. This chapter covers the basics of what you need to know to create great queries that will make an agent or editor cry tears of joy. You will also learn how to put together a synopsis and book proposal.

The Submission Process

The submission process is not the time to flap your creative wings. You want to impress the recipient with your writing skills and your ability to follow directions. To start, carefully read the agent or publisher's submission guidelines.

If you're writing a novel, an agent or publisher will usually request a query letter, a book synopsis, and the complete manuscript. For nonfiction, expect to submit a query letter, a book proposal, and sample chapters.

Let's assume you have read the submission guidelines and are ready to move forward. This chapter explains the different parts of your pitch package.

Cover Letter

Don't forget to include a cover letter with your submission package. Agents and editors receive thousands of queries a month; you can't expect them to remember every Zoe, Lucas, and Mia they have requested information from. You need to gently remind them who you are. Here are some tips for writing your cover letter from "The Rock-Solid Submission Package" by Blythe Camenson and Marshal J. Cook:

Who are you again? Remind the agent where you met and that you are following up on a request for more information. If you had additional communication with the agent since the initial meeting, remind them also of these exchanges.

Did someone refer you to the agent? Agents may not remember who referred you, even if you mentioned it during your initial interaction, so be sure to mention again.

What's your manuscript about? It may seem like all agents have short-term memory loss, but you'll have to remind the agent what your manuscript is about. A few sentences should be sufficient. Be sure to include the name of your book, an expected word count, the book's genre, and a one-sentence summary.

The Pitch Package

An agent or publisher will expect you to follow guidelines when pitching your project. Again, check their website for details. There are common elements you can expect to submit when pitching your book idea. Let's take a closer look at each one.

The query letter

When you send a query, you want to stand out, but in a good way. Some writers use gimmicks, but they end up looking foolish and unprofessional. Maya Rock writes in the April 2008 issue of *The Writer* ("The Do's and Don'ts of Agent Queries") that some writers slip goodies, like cookies, into the envelope, hoping to impress a potential agent. Other authors write their query in the voice of the main character. It never works and brands you as an amateur.

Rock also advises against trying to sell yourself to an agent. Your goal is to sell your work. Rock says, "The focus of the letter should be on getting the agent to fall in love with your book, not you."[48]

Think of your query letter as a sales pitch. You have one chance to make a good impression. Your goal is get the agent or publish to request additional information. Agents and editors receive tons of queries each month. Unfortunately, a large percentage of these queries are rejected. You may have a wonderful novel or book idea but if your query sucks, you have zero probability of an agent or editor requesting additional information. Fortunately, you have this guide to help you craft the perfect query letter.

Here are some tips to keep in mind:

- **Do not** send sample pages, a complete manuscript or any material with your query letter *unless* the agent or publisher's guidelines say it's okay.

- You may have five book projects, but please don't pitch more than one idea at a time.

---

48. Rock, 2008.

- Keep your query letter to one page.

- Use single spacing, and an easily readable font like Times New Roman or Courier, set at 10- or 12-point, with 1-inch margins.

- Mention if you have photos or illustrations that would work well with your book.

- Address the editor as Mr. or Ms., unless you are unsure. For example, for unisex names or initials only, address without Mr. or Ms. Don't address your query "To Whom It May Concern", "Gentlemen", "Agent", "Editor" or any other generic greeting. If you're unsure, double check contact information. Definitely don't get cozy and address the recipient by his or her first name or be too informal ("Hi", for example).

- **Do not** call an agent or editor to pitch your idea over the phone.

- Most agents and publishers prefer e-mail queries but be sure to check the guidelines. If you are sending your query via snail mail, don't use fancy schmancy stationary. Or worse, your old *Hello Kitty* stationary from ten years ago. A query letter is a business transaction and should be treated as such.

- **Do not** compare yourself to well-known writers. No matter what your grandma says, you are not the next J.K. Rowling or the reincarnated soul of F. Scott Fitzgerald.

- Please don't threaten to take your work to another agent or publisher, or demand they read your manuscript or proposal. Boy (or girl) bye. You'll sound like a whiny baby. Also, don't tell the agent or editor he or she will miss out on a good thing if they don't represent you or publish your work of literary greatness.

Parts of a query letter

Your query letter should contain four parts: the opening hook, supporting details, the writer's bio, and the conclusion.

The opening hook

The first introductory paragraph is where you hook the agent or editor. You have to entice the receiver into wanting to read more. If you can establish a connection with the agent or editor with the first sentence, there's a good chance your query will get a full read.

Other ways to connect include a reminder that you met the agent or publisher at a conference (or heard them speak), someone referred you to them, or you are responding to a call for queries. If your work is similar to clients they represent or books they have published, it's okay to tell the agent or editor you believe your project is a good fit.

When writing your opening, always focus on the positive. Don't say you have queried X number of agents or editors and been turned down by all of them. Also, don't display any doubt through your writing that your query will get rejected. Be confident, but not arrogant.

Next, you want to briefly explain your project. You should be able to explain your idea in one succinct sentence and include the topic or genre, your book's title, and length.

Supporting details

Now that you have hooked the agent or editor, you want to expand on your project with supporting details. This section should also be brief—one or two paragraphs.

If you are writing a novel, summarize your story. For non-fiction writers, offer additional details on the topic that shows you have a well-thought-out plan. For example, you could mention who you plan to interview or any bibliographic information you plan to use. You can also mention the book's target audience or why the topic is important or timely.

In this section include a statement showing the benefit of publishing your novel or non-fiction book. You need to explain to the agent or editor what makes your story not only unique, but interesting. If your query is a snooze fest, your manuscript will probably bore readers.

The writer's bio

Why are you the person to write this book? This is a question the agent or editor will ask before deciding whether to proceed. In this section, you discuss your qualifications. It's okay if you have never published before — just don't dwell on it. You should connect your experiences to the topic you are writing about. If you are pitching a non-fiction project, you have to convince the editor or publisher that you can finish the manuscript.

As a new writer, you may not have much (if any) publishing credits. Make sure to list all of your writer qualifications including personal blogs, writing for your school's newspaper or creating the weekly newsletter for your church. Also include any contests or awards you have won. If you are a member of a professional writing organization, include this information also.

Don't forget to include any hobbies or work experience that's relevant to your book idea. If you have experience working as a summer camp counselor and you are writing a book about summer camp, this could work in your favor.

The conclusion

In sales, there's a term referred to as a "call to action". This is where the salesperson tells the target exactly what they want them to do next. "Buy my widget," for example. In your query, your conclusion should have a call to action. You want the agent or editor to request more information. But first, since I know your parents taught you manners, don't forget to thank the recipient for taking time to read your query. Then you should ask if you can send your manuscript or proposal. I know it seems like they would assume that's what you want but this is a business transaction and you should follow procedure.

Synopsis

A synopsis summarizes your novel, touching on the major events and introduces the characters. What's the ideal length of a synopsis? Writers are typically encouraged to create two versions. A short synopsis is about two pages, while the longer version is usually no more than eight pages. You should have both versions because you won't know which one an agent may request.

Agents and editors may request a synopsis with the query letter or afterwards. Make sure to read the guidelines because an agent or editor may request a shorter or longer synopsis, and you will have to make adjustmentsm accordingly.

What an Agent Looks for in a Synopsis

If an agent or editor is interested in your book project based on your awesome query, the next step is to read your synopsis. Why not request the full manuscript? Because a perfectly crafted synopsis will help an agent or editor decide if your novel has potential. If you can't put together a compelling synopsis, chances are your novel won't be well-written either.

After reading your synopsis, the agent or editor will decide if he or she wants to read the complete manuscript. Some of the things they look for include:

- **Your writing ability.** Are you a strong writer? Does your writing grab and hold the reader's attention?

- **Your voice.** Are you writing in your own distinctive voice or trying to copy another writer?

- **Do you understand your genre?** If you promised sci-fi, your novel shouldn't read more like a comedy.

- **Will the story engage readers?** Many synopses have great promise but fall flat in execution. An agent or editor will read the complete manuscript to make sure the novel is a page turner and not one that will quickly get tossed aside when it starts to waver.

How to Write an Effective Synopsis

Your synopsis should leave the reader wanting more— more of your manuscript, that is. Here are some useful tips to keep mind while you craft your synopsis.

- **Write in narrative format**. A synopsis is not a summary in the traditional sense. It should not read like an English 101 assignment. You should write in the third person, using present tense. Don't include any lists or bulleted points.

- **Condense the story**. You only have a few pages to tell your story, so focus on the main characters and important plot points. Leave minor characters and sub-plots for the full manuscript read.

- **Include emotional turning points**. Include events that show how your protagonist develops and transforms overtime.

- **Use your writer voice.** Your synopsis should mimic the voice and tone of your book. If you're writing a thriller, the synopsis should convey a sense of suspense. If your book is humorous, the tone of the synopsis should be the same.

- **Create compelling sketches of the main characters.** What makes you decide to read one book over another? The description of the book's main character usually draws readers in, begging for more. When creating your synopsis, describe your main characters so an agent or editor wants to get to know them better.

- **Don't end on a cliffhanger.** This may work for the season finale of your favorite TV program but not for a synopsis. The agent or editor needs to know how the story ends. Not revealing the ending is the quickest way to get rejected. In the conclusion of your synopsis, you need to resolve the basic plot points and explain what happened to the main characters.

Proposals

One of the benefits of writing a nonfiction book is you won't have to write the full manuscript before you sell the idea. But don't think you get off easy. In order to sell your book idea you'll need to do your homework. You need to put together a banging proposal that entices an agent to take you on as a client and an editor to buy your idea.

You can expect to write a few sample chapters that will go along with your proposal, so you're not completely off the writing hook. Still, it's better to invest a few weeks or months writing a few chapters and creating your proposal than to spend years writing a book that may never sell. The exception to this rule is narrative non-fiction, such as memoirs; publishers usually ask for the completed manuscript instead of a proposal.

The Purpose of a Book Proposal

Your proposal should be well-written. It's your only chance to sell your idea, so please don't rush. It may take several weeks to perfect your proposal; it will be worth it in the end when you get a book deal. Your book proposal should:

- Introduce your book's topic

- Show why you're qualified to write the book

- Showcase your superb writing skills through sample chapters

- Provide a market analysis of books similar to yours

- Include logistical information: length and format (sidebars, expert, interviews, photos, and charts), etc.

- Convince the reader there's a market for your book

- Highlight your writer's platform, and present your ideas for marketing and promoting your book

Each month agents and editors review thousands of proposals hoping to find one with potential. Your proposal can be that one. How? Follow these tips on creating a perfect book proposal.

Components of a book proposal

The length of your proposal will vary, but expect to write 12 to 40 pages. This does not include the sample chapter(s), so add another 10 to 20 pages. A book proposal should include the following sections:

The title page: A good title can win over an editor or agent or lead to rejection. Use subtitles when necessary to explain ambiguous titles. Avoid head-scratching titles that don't relate to the books content, theme or subject matter. The title you submit is known as the "working title". As noted earlier in this guide, ultimately the title is determined by the publisher — don't get too attached to the one you choose.

The proposal's table of contents: Include a table of contents after the title page that lists each section of the proposal. Align the section header to the left and the page number to the right.

The overview: The overview summarizes your book and is usually one to three concise paragraphs. In "Landing the Six-Figure Deal: What Makes Your Proposal Hot", in the *Writer's Market 2017*, SJ Hodges suggests writing the first draft of your overview after the table of contents and chapter outlines. "You'll know much more about the content and scope of your material even if you're not 100 percent certain about the voice and tone."[49] After you finish the sample chapters, Hodges suggest returning to the overview to edit as necessary.

In addition to presenting a case why your book is important, the overview should:

- Include any information on special features you would like to use — sidebars, images, charts, quizzes, case studies, etc.

- Discuss the overall structure of the book — an explanation of the parts, chapters, and sections

- Give an estimated word and page count, and delivery date

A competitive analysis: Agents and editors want to know how your book idea stacks up against similar titles. For the answer, they look to a competitive analysis. Sorry, but you'll have to do more — you guessed it — home-

---

49. Hodges, 2016.

work. For your competitive analysis, you'll review and compare your brilliant book idea to a handful of similar books already on the market.

Choose five to 10 similar titles for your analysis. If your topic is specialized, you can probably choose fewer books. Don't write that you couldn't find any comparable books. The agent or editor will either assume you took the easy (lazy) way out— because he or she will know that books on most topics exist — or if for some odd reason there aren't any books on your chosen subject, then perhaps the idea is way too weird to publish.

You can find titles by visiting Amazon.com and running a keyword search based on your topic. The "Look Inside" feature is a great way to have a peek at the table of contents to see which topics are covered. You can also preview available free content, but for the books you plan to compare you should purchase the books or check them out from your library to complete your analysis.

Be sure to include the following information in your analysis:

- Bibliographic information—book title, author, publisher, year of publication, page count, price, available formats (print, e-book), and the ISBN number

- An assessment of how well the book delivers on its promises

- An explanation of what differentiates your book's goals from your competitors' titles

- A concluding summary of why your book is better than the comparable titles

Include key reasons why your book is more interesting or useful, but don't bash the book or insult the author.

The promotional and marketing plan: In this section, explain why your book should be published. Who will buy this book? The agent or editor will want to see a clear answer to this important question. If you fail to adequately answer it, your proposal will probably get rejected.

As mentioned earlier in this guide, writers are expected to help promote and market their books. In your proposal, you must show a potential agent or editor you have ideas for promoting your book. Your publisher's marketing department will have ideas of their own, but your plan may offer fresh ideas on how to best promote your book.

The plan should be detailed, specific, and most of all, realistic.

Good example:

"I will create a book trailer that will appear on my website, which receives 25,000 unique visitors a month. The trailer will also appear on my YouTube channel which currently has 50,000 subscribers."

Bad (vague, unrealistic) example:

"I will promote my book on all of the talk shows, and morning entertainment programs."

Audience: You have to prove there's an audience for your book *and* that it's large enough to justify publishing it. Resist the temptation to say your book is for "everyone". Be specific and identify exactly who the target audience is.

You can also include statistical information, talk about the popularity of similar titles, or cite recent case studies or reports. In this section you should also mention ideas for potential spin-offs or serialization, although it is not necessary to sell your idea.

About the author: This section helps sell you as the person qualified to bring the book to life. Include your platform (more on platforms in the next chapter) and any favorable information about you to prove you are capable of writing a book.

The chapter outline: Your chapters should have a tentative title. Like book titles, this may change, but for now, include a working title for each chapter. Include a table of contents for the book, followed by the chapter summaries. The text should be written in narrative format like mini chapters, instead of writing, "I will show . . .", etc.

The section is a preview of your book and presents to the agent or editor the information you plan to cover—and most importantly, how you plan to deliver it. If you are all over the place, jumping from topic to topic in a haphazard manner, you can expect a rejection. On the other hand, if you can logically lay out your plan, you will at least get serious consideration.

Sample chapters: If you create a winning proposal but your sample chapters fall flat then you have wasted a lot of time and energy trying to get a book deal that probably will never happen. So make sure your sample chapters prove you have the writing chops to deliver on your promise.

The sample chapters should showcase your writing skills and give the reader a preview of what to expect from a full manuscript. How many chapters should you include? This is a question only the agent or editor can answer. Each will have different guidelines but you can expect to submit a few chapters or 25-30 pages.

Supplemental material: You can also include any favorable material along with your submission, such as letters or copies of articles written about you. You can include a professional headshot or videos of any TV or speaking appearances. If you have published any articles or won writing contests, include that information here. As a young adult, you may not have a lot of material that would fit in this category, but if you do be sure to include it. Anything that paints a bright picture of you should be included.

Now that you know how to create your winning pitch package, you should begin to work on your author platform. The next chapter will show you exactly how.

Chapter 7: *Your Author Platform*

It's not enough to have a great idea for a book — agents and editors look at an author's platform before deciding whether to represent him or her or offer a book deal. It seems that lately it's becoming more important to establish a platform but some writers are confused by the term "platform". This definition by author and editor Jane Friedman should clear up any confusion. She writes that an author's platform is ". . . an ability to sell books because of who you are or who you can reach." [50]

Your platform includes potential avenues you use that could attract readers for your book. You should start working on your platform before you write the first word of your novel, or begin researching ideas for a non-fiction book.

Your platform includes all the ways you are visible. The higher your visibility, the greater your chances of attracting potential readers. It takes time to grow your base, which is why you should start as soon as you decide to write your book. If you have not already started, that's okay —you can still catch up.

So what are some examples of writer platforms? Any method you use to reach an audience including a website, blog, newsletter, video, or YouTube channel. The following sections discuss ways you can develop your platform.

---

50. Friedman, 2017.

Branding

Your brand establishes your author identity. It includes how you present yourself to readers and distinguish yourself from other writers. If you can show an agent or editor that your brand is already strong, you increase the chance of getting the green light on your project.

Branding includes who you are *and* how you want to be perceived by readers (authoritative, quirky, etc.). Your brand should also trigger emotions. In "How to Develop an Effective Author Brand", published in the 2017 *Writer's Market*, Leslie Lee Sanders writes: "If someone were to describe you and your brand, what words or emotion would you like them to use?"[51]

Once you decide on your trigger words, use them in all of your content including books, your website, blogs, tweets, and Facebook posts. Triggering a reader's emotions is only the first step; you have to make good on your promise and do so consistently. This consistency helps establish our brand.

If an author promises to scare the pants off me, that's what I expect to happen. Well, maybe not literally, but you get the point.

In Seller's article, she says brand building is a four- cycle process: make a promise, deliver, build trust, and repeat. Here is an example of how it works.

An author makes a promise: Triggers my emotions by telling me:

> "Hey reader, this book will scare your pants off!"

Deliver: I read the book and I am so scared my pants (figuratively) fly off

---

51. Sanders, 2016.

Build Trust: Author: *"Psst*, hey reader, here's another scary book for ya!"

Repeat: Since the author delivered on the previous promise, I now trust this book will also give me chills, so my response is an enthusiastic: "Okay!"

Part of building your brand includes developing your own distinctive voice. Loyal readers expect your books to reflect the voice they associate with you. Mary Buckham writes in "8 Elements to Amplify Your Author Brand," published in the *Novel & Short Story Writer's Market 2017* that branding is ". . . what readers think and feel when they hear or read your name on a book."[52]

She also points out that every book is not for every reader and knowing who your potential readers are can help develop your brand. If you write whimsical books for young readers, then your brand shouldn't project a serious tone. If you can identify who your potential readers are, you can develop your brand and effectively reach those readers. Your readers then become a community. The stronger your brand, the stronger your community.

Buckham discusses a way authors can help their brand by creating an "Origin Story". This is the story of how you became a writer. Make sure the story you tell is consistent or you might tarnish your brand. If a reader hears you tell the story at one event and then you tell a different story at another event, trust is broken because who knows which story is correct.

Your brand also includes communication style and delivery, writes Buckham. How well does an author interact with readers? Do readers only hear from an author when a new book is about to be released? The answers to these questions shapes an author's communication style.

---

52. Buckham, 2016.

Delivery includes how authors interact with their audience when face-to-face. Does the author sign books, barely glancing up? When giving a reading, does he or she read from a stack of constantly shuffled papers, not looking up until it's time for the Q & A? Oh, I have a question for you — why are so boring?

How readers communicate with their fans is crucial to developing a positive brand image. Image also includes visuals used in your books that are associated with your character or images associated with you. For example, the image I have of *Game of Thrones* author George R.R. Martin, is a rotund Santa Clause-ish man with suspenders and a little black cap.

Creating a Website

Another nagging question you may have is whether you should have a website. I suppose you could manage without one, but most agents, editors, and your fans will expect you to have one.

You can hire someone to design and maintain your site, but it's easy to create your own. The first step is to register your domain name. A domain name is the name that comes before the .com, .net, .org, etc. in a website's address. Try to get your legal name if possible or the name you plan to use as a writer. Registering a domain is inexpensive. Even if you're not ready to create a website today, you should register your domain name. Go ahead, I'll wait.

Okay, now that we have that taken care of, let's talk about some of the things you should put on your website. Author J.A. Konrath says your site should be "sticky" meaning the content should be good enough to make people want to stick around and read more. He wrote about websites in the October 2007 issue of *Writer's Digest* ("Sling Your Web"), where he encourages authors to create websites for individual book titles. Of course, you need to do this once you're sure of the title. To draw traffic to your website, include a link in emails, on message boards, and in social media posts.

What should your website include?

The final decision is up to you, but here are some items you should include:

- Reviews, interviews, and testimonials

- Book excerpts

- A headshot/photos

- Links to your social media profiles

- An "About Me" Page

- Your Contact Info

- Writing samples

- A link for purchasing your book(s)

- An events calendar

- Current and future projects

You need to have a strategy when designing your website, says Karen Rider in the September 2012 issue of *The Writer* ("Make Your Homepage POP: Follow These Basic Principles to Book Your Web Traffic"). Part of that strategy is making sure visitors react, whether it's clicking on a link to purchase your book or hiring you for a freelance writing gig.

Other ways to make sure your website pops, according to Rider:

- Include an image of your book's cover and a short synopsis

- If you are selling your writing services, you need a short bio that will convince editors to hire you

- Don't put too much copy on your homepage and make sure the information is not boring

- Don't put too many images or graphics because they take too long to load

- Include share buttons (Facebook, Twitter, etc.)

Where to get design ideas

When looking for design ideas it's okay to check out other websites to see what works for you and what drives you crazy. I hate pop-ups, videos set to auto-play, and a site with a lot of moving parts. The things that annoy you will probably irritate visitors to your site, so skip elaborate bells and whistles.

Barbara Demarco-Barrett's article "Build Your Website" (*Writer's Yearbook 2007),* reminds writers to update their site often to remove stale information. Things you can leave up include book excerpts, reviews, and clips (published articles). You should take down old information like notices for events that have long passed.

Blogging instead of having a website

Instead of creating full-fledged websites, many writers decide to blog. You can choose to have a blog in addition to or instead of a regular website. Should you blog? This is a personal decision based on whether you think you have time to blog consistently.

Blogs are a good choice for some writers because they are easier to update than a website and usually easier to imbed video, audio, and other effects.

If you don't have writing credits, having a blog is a good way to showcase your talents as you build your portfolio and platform. If you plan to freelance, for example, editors can read your blog to get a feel for your writing abilities.

If you create good content, you can build a following which will help you when you're looking for an agent or editor because you already have a built-in fan base. Fiction writers can blog about their genre or publishing experiences, post short stories, interview guest writers, or conduct reviews. You should comment on other authors' blogs, and write guest posts to continue to increase traffic to your site.

Social Networking

A social network is an online platform that allows users to connect with others. Writers use social networking as part of their platform and can include the following:

Podcasts

A podcast distributes audio files over the Internet. Authors can use podcasts to serialize their novels, discuss writing, read excerpts from an upcoming book, or launch their own radio show.

Nancy Hendrickson writes in "Use Podcasts to Promote Your Book," (*The Writer,* November 2007), that a podcast can turn listeners into buyers because they get the chance to know the writer on a personal level.

Creating a podcast is not difficult. If your computer has a built-in microphone, that's all you need. If not, buy one, plug it in, and you're ready to go. Next, record your message, convert the file to MP3 format, upload to the Internet and that's it — you officially have a podcast.

You can upload to your website, blog, or use a hosting site. If you build a large audience, you can impress an agent or editor with your ability to keep humans entertained.

You can test podcasting and make a few dollars in the process. Just upload your podcast to podiobooks.com, a site where users can listen for free. If they decide to make a donation, 75 percent of the money goes to the writer.

Want to start your own radio show? You can use a free or paid service like blogcastradio.com, where you can discuss your book, interview guests, and even have commercials.

The Big Two: Facebook and Twitter

The two most popular social networking sites are undoubtedly Facebook and Twitter. Most people seem to gravitate to one or the other, although some are equally active on both. How can you get the most out of your time of these two sites? Here are some tips from the staff at *Writer's Digest,* from "A Writer's Guide to Social Networking" (*Writer's Digest,* May/June 2009).

Facebook:

- Join groups related to your subject or genre. Better yet, start your own group.

- Use the "post events feature" to invite your friends or group members to attend events like book signings, readings, etc.

Twitter:

- Follow people that can be beneficial to your writing career, like agents, publishers, other writers, etc.

- Have a tweet plan. What are your goals? Do you want to drive traffic to your website, attract the attention of potential readers, agents, or other publishing connections? Or are you tweeting just for fun?

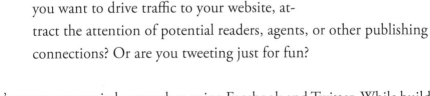

It's easy to get carried away when using Facebook and Twitter. While building your platform, you should set a specific amount of time to spend on each and when your time is up, you should get back to writing or building your platform on other channels. You can also use a scheduling service like Hootsuite (www.hootsuite.com) that will send your tweets and posts out at certain times. All you have to do is create the posts, schedule them for a particular time, and Hootsuite will send them out for you. It's like having your own social media manager. It also stops you from spending too much time on these platforms when you need to write.

Online Chats

An online chat is kind of a visual podcast. Chats allow writers to connect with their audience in real-time. For shy writers, chats are a godsend. Make sure you use a service that will record the chat for those who missed it. You can use a chat hosting site or use services like Google Hangouts or Facebook Live.

Author MaryJanice Davidson ("A Friendly Chat Pays Dividends." *The Writer* (April 2002), offers these tips for writers interested in hosting a chat:

- Why are you chatting? Do you have a new release? Would you like to talk about your writing aspirations? Do you want readers to learn more about your characters? Or do you want to do a Q & A?

- Practice beforehand by thinking of questions viewers may ask.

- Offer something free

Creating a Pinterest Board

Pinterest is a site that allows users to share their likes with others. Why not make a board for yourself, a character from your book or your book's topic?

Laura DiSilverio offers these handy tips for creating a board ("Pinterest is Worth a Thousand Words. "*Writer's Digest* (September 2012)

- Build a board that represents who you are as a writer or build a board around a character. Suppose your main characters loves expensive items. You could create a board and pin items you imagine he or she would like.

- Nonfiction writers can build boards based on their research or add supplemental material that didn't make it into the book.

- Writing a memoir? Create a board and upload pictures from your childhood or pin items that stir childhood memories.

- Link your boards to other social media accounts – on your website, blogs, and in your e-mail's signature line.

- Unlike other social media outlets, Pinterest is visual; there are no conversations. However, you can add descriptive captions,which allows readers to understand the back-story of why you choose a particular image.

Book trailers

Many authors are jumping on the book trailer bandwagon. A book trailer is similar to a movie trailer. It's short video of what your book is about. Book trailers entice viewers to read your book in the same way a movie trailer will cause you to plunk down $12.50 at the movies or pay $2.99 to watch it on Amazon Video.

If you want to create a trailer for your book, follow these tips:

- The video should grab the viewer's attention in a few seconds

- The trailer should be brief— 1 to 3 minutes

- The video can be intriguing, informational, or entertaining

- You can video yourself or someone reading an excerpt or show a still image of your book's cover or other relevant image

- Play appropriate mood music in the background

- A fun idea for non-fiction books is to have someone (you?) act out a scene

After you create your trailer, you can upload it to your website or put it on your own YouTube channel. Be sure to include links to your trailer in your email and on social media. If you are having a book signing, bring a computer along to play the trailer. This is a great way to entice stragglers to come on over. You can also display the trailer if you are giving a reading, if the venue has a display you can connect to that is.

Creating your YouTube channel

Having a YouTube channel gives you a place to load your videos, podcasts, and book trailers. Your channel can direct visitors to your website. This can help increase traffic and build your brand.

Your YouTube videos can show an editor or agent how you would perform on television. Recording a video can help shy writers get comfy before having to do live events.

What types of videos can you shoot? Whatever you like. You can read book excerpts, interview other writers, or talk about your writing life. You can have someone act out a scene from your book, if you like.

Creating a YouTube channel is easy. Do you have a Google account? Then you already have a channel. If not, take a few minutes and create an account.

To access your channel, sign in. You should see a "My Channel" tab. Click on it to open your channel's dashboard. You can customize your channel by adding background art or images and a description of your channel. You can change the settings to your satisfaction and allow as much or as little public viewing as you like.

To upload a video, click on "video manager", then click the upload icon, located in the top right side of your screen, next to the notifications bell. It looks like an "up" arrow. Follow the instructions and you're on your way.

Viewers will see your uploads and if you want, you can allow visitors a peek inside your private life. By changing your settings, viewers can see which videos you have "liked", the channels you subscribe to, and view your playlist.

By allowing public access, your fans find out who your favorite singers are, the type of music you like, and what makes you giggle. YouTube also allows you to livestream, among numerous other features.

Book Signings, Readings, and Tours

If you want people to buy your book, at some point you are probably going to have to participate in a book signing or reading. You may also have to tour to promote your book. This section will prepare you for these types of events, so don't worry.

Planning your event

Author Gigi Rosenberg recounts the horror of her first book reading in the October 2007 issue of *Writer's Digest* ("Marketing: Give a Good Reading"), including a runny nose and an out-of-body feeling. After that disastrous first reading, she vowed to never give a bad reading again. She developed a plan she suggests authors following in the weeks leading up to the reading.

Two weeks before: Rosenberg suggests rehearsing with a friend — if possible in the event space. Have your friend introduce you and time the reading. Don't forget to do a Q & A!

If you're going to stand during the reading, you should stand while practicing. If you're using a podium during the reading, use one during your practice run, if possible.

The week before: Call the venue to confirm you will arrive 45 minutes to an hour before the reading. This gives you time to check out the room. When you call, also confirm who will introduce you, how long the reading and Q & A is, and where you'll sign books.

The big day: The big day has finally arrived and you're in the venue at least 45 minutes early. It's time to get comfy with the space. Rosenberg suggests you walk around the room, sit in the audience, and familiarize yourself with the microphone. You want to make sure there's water nearby and that you have some tissue in your pocket.

During your reading it's important to relax and speak in a natural, conversational tone. If you need water, drink it and ask for more if necessary. How many times have you attended an event and a few noisy strays waltz in late? It's distracting for the audience; can you imagine how distracting it is for the speaker? If this happens to you, stop reading, welcome the latecomers, and then continue with the reading. If someone slips in quietly, Rosenberg suggests you don't pause your reading.

When you are finished, don't forget to thank your host and your audience. If the host didn't, you should direct the audience to the location of your signing.

Rosenberg suggests some items you should bring with you, including the book you plan to read from or a copy of the section printed in 14-point font, and a small watch or clock. You can also bring a lucky charm and don't forget your glasses. I wear reading glasses, which I lose often, so I always have at least two extra pair with me at all times: one in my car and a spare pair in my purse.

Author J.A. Konraith offers some great tips on planning your book signing. In "Book-Signing Success", appearing in the June 2007 issue of *Writer's Digest*, Konraith's plan starts a month before the event. The plan is proactive—the author takes the lead in arranging the signings. His ideas are for bookstore signings but could work for other venues. Here are a few of Konraith's tips:

A month before:

- Contact or drop by the venue to speak with the manager or event coordinator. Warning: you may have to convince the store to host your signing.

- If you are with a small publisher, plan on possibly bringing the books yourself or offer the bookseller the standard 40% discount.

- Larger publishers may supply the books and pay a co-op fee to the store (money to host the event). If they refuse to pay, the store probably won't host the event.

Two weeks before:

- If all goes well, start advertising your event. Make your own fliers and send them to the bookstore, list the event on your website, social media account, etc.

- Make a large poster with your book's cover and a sign that reads, "Author Event Today." Your publisher may handle this for you. Also, the bookstore may have the author event sign but just in case, you should have your own.

Three days before:

Call the store to make sure they have your books in stock; if not, offer to bring your own copies.

The day of:

- Arrive at the venue early and introduce yourself to the staff. Konraith suggests bringing donuts or pizza for the employees. You should talk to each member and give a summary of your book, so they can sing your praises to customers.

- How should you dress? Business casual or better. Don't look like you rolled out of bed and decided to stop by. Konraith also suggests wearing a nametag with "AUTHOR" written on it.

- If possible, try to get a table at the front of the store. However, you should walk around and introduce yourself.

- When you are trying to hand sell your book, use a soft sell approach. Don't hound or harass customers.

- Be sure to thank customers whether they buy your book or not. Pass out business cards. Even if a customer does not buy your book on the spot, he or she may visit your website, read about you, and decide to buy your book.

- If the store has a PA system, ask the staff to announce your presence every 30 minutes or make the announcement yourself.

- How long should you stay? Konraith suggests at least four hours. If the store is busy you can stay up to six hours.

- After you finish, if the store has any unsold books, ask if you can sign them and if they have a "signed copy" or similar sticker.

Drive-by Signings

Konraith has an interesting twist on the traditional book signings. He calls it drive-by signings. Publishers and bookstores have a particular set of rules concerning book signings. This method works well for stores that can't have "official" signings or when you want to cover a lot of territory in a short period. The idea is to go to a bookstore, sign all your books, get out and then on to the next store. Here's how it works:

- Locate stores within 50 miles of your home or a location you plan to visit

- Contact the stores to find out if they carry your book, and if so, ask how many they have in stock. **This is important**: Don't tell the store you're the author because of the rules related to book signings.

- If the store has enough of your books, create a map of the ones you want to visit. Konraith says he wouldn't make a trip to sign a few paperbacks, but he would for hard covers, which usually sell out.

- When you arrive at the store, find your books and bring them to the counter. Explain to the employee who you are and ask if it's okay to sign your books. Be prepared for one of two reactions. The employee will be excited that a famous writer stopped by and will enthusiastically welcome you. Or he or she will look at you like you have two heads. Either way, sign your books so you can move on to the next store. If they have "autographed copy" stickers, slap one on each book.

- If possible, meet with each employee and ask him or her to read your book. If they like it, they could be your biggest cheerleader.

- Keep a record of your travels. Then send the information to your agent or publisher (or include it in your pitch package when trying to lure a new one).

- Return to each store (if possible) a few months later to sign any more stock that has arrived since your last visit.

A one-hour book reading plan

When you have a reading, it's normal to feel nervous. One way to feel better is to make sure you have a plan. In her article, "Going Public: How to Ace Readings, Singings, Interviews & More," published in the September 2013 issue of *Writer's Digest,* Elizabeth Sims presents a plan for a managing a one-hour reading.

5 minutes: An introduction by the host, appropriate thank-yous (from you to the host and audience)

10-15 minutes: Introduce the text you're going to read, then proceed with the reading

10-15 minutes: Talk about yourself (Remember the origin story?) and your book

10-15 minutes: Q & A; thank-yous again to the host and audience

10-15 minutes: Sign your books

Some writers prefer to talk about themselves and the book first and then proceed to the reading. You can change this order if you like. Sims adds that if you have a small audience, you should put the chairs in a circle instead of standing at a podium or sitting at a table, speaking to a nearly empty hall. But don't make a big deal about the low turnout.

When you have a book signing, keep your fingers crossed that customers walk away with armloads of your books. In "Book Signings Add Up to Book Sales," appearing in the August 2006 edition of *The Writer,* Carolyn

Campbell suggests that if you have a book related to a specific holiday, try to arrange a signing the weekend before. Sales are usually higher because customers are buying gifts. For example, if you have a book about mothers and daughters, try to arrange a signing before Mother's Day. A book of love poems would do well before Valentine's Day. You should also try to make your signing an event if possible—a demonstration for a cookbook or craft book, for example.

Campbell also reminds authors to schedule media appearances by contacting local radio stations to see if they would be interested in interviewing you. Or call the local morning news or other local programs to see if there's any interest. If your book covers an issue that is currently in the news or of local interest, you have a better chance of getting interviews.

Unusual venues

Have you attended a book signing, reading or author event? Chances are the venue was a bookstore, store, library, or part of literary event. If you are thinking these are the only places you should schedule an appearance, you are missing out on untapped opportunities to reach customers. Check out these unusual and often overlooked venues:

- Senior centers and retirement communities
- A church, synagogue, or other house of worship
- Businesses, government offices
- Supermarkets, big box stores
- Museums and other attractions
- Virtual readings/signings (people who purchase books during your reading or signing will get an autographed copy mailed to them)

- Pop up signings/readings in public spaces, like parks

- Private events in a relative or friend's home

You can have an event almost anywhere, especially venues relating to the topic of your book. Does your book prominently feature a pet? Hold an event in a pet shop, vet's office or dog wash. Is the main character in your book a magician? Check out a magic shop. Did you write a picture book? Try a pediatrician's office, beauty salon or barbershop.

If your book is food-related, try bakeries and restaurants. When you use your imagination, you will find there is an unlimited number of venues you can approach.

CASE STUDY: NIHAR SUTHAR

Imagine that you have toiled incredibly hard for months, or even years, to publish your book. Now that it's finally released, you're basking in all the glory. Little do you know that the real journey is only beginning. Once your book is live, you have to market it and make sure readers know it even exists. There are countless ways to promote your book, one of which is going on a book tour. Many people in the publishing industry may tell you that the days of the classic book tour are over. However, I'm here to tell you that they are still alive and well; if you plan and execute it properly, you can derive several benefits from a book tour.

So, how do you go about actually planning one? My tactics are a bit different. Rather than targeting the traditional bookstores, I instead go where I know I will always have an audience. For example, I recently wrote a book titled *The Corridor of Uncertainty*. When I went on tour to promote it, I could have easily arranged visits at every bookstore in North America, South America, and Asia where I planned to go. However, since I'm a relatively unknown author, it's unlikely that anybody would have actually showed up at my "book signing events." One breakthrough that I had about my book, though, is that it is a perfect educational read for high school students. It blends together sports, politics, religion, history, and culture in the Middle East region — topics that are sometimes covered in classes.

I started compiling a list of high schools in the countries where I wanted to tour (based on where cricket was a popular sport), and then sent the teachers there quick emails with a few compelling reasons about why supplementing their curriculum with my book would be beneficial. I also offered to visit the schools and speak to the students about my inspirations, so they could all personally connect with the author. For every 20 or 30 emails I sent out, I got one or two responses. This may not seem too impressive, but what happened in those one or two responses was magical. The teachers not only asked me to supply 40-50 books for their students to purchase, but they also fully covered the expenses of my travel so I could go visit the schools.

Effectively, my tour was free. I had an unforgettable experience going into schools and speaking to hundreds of students. At every event, I had a guaranteed audience that I could engage right in front of me. What did I take away from the entire tour? Sometimes, you have to think outside the box. Don't believe that you have to only visit bookstores on a tour. If you are an unknown author, build your brand by thinking of other relevant audiences that you can easily engage. Arrange your book tour around those channels. I promise that you will have more success.

Nihar Suthar is an award-winning writer, covering inspirational stories around the world. He strives to publish works that break the status quo. Suthar was born in Lewistown, Pennsylvania, and graduated from Cornell University in January 2016.

How to give a good reading even if you are terrified

I'm not shy, but I don't necessarily like speaking in front of unfamiliar faces. It's not because I lack confidence—I hate the sound of my high-pitched, squeaky voice. When I'm excited it gets squeakier. But when I have to speak in public, I do so without any fear or anxiety.

As a published author, you may be asked to give a reading. Will you be prepared to? Author Deborah Prum writes, "Some people lack the confidence to give a reading because they lack confidence in themselves as a writer."[53]

In her article, "How to Give a Good Reading," published in the May 2001 issue of *The Writer*, Prum writes that authors should identify what terrifies

---

53. Prum, 2001.

them the most about giving a reading. Next, imagine the worst-case scenario and think it through to a logical conclusion. For instance, if you lose your place or inadvertently say a word you didn't intend to say which causes giggles from the audience. What happens next? After the audience settles down, you move on.

"Making a mistake is not the end of the world,"[54] Prum writes. You can lessen your fear of public readings by following these tips, according to Prum:

- Practice and if possible, videotape yourself

- Be expressive without being overly dramatic

- Know your material well enough that you don't have to read without looking up from the page periodically

- When choosing your material, it should be able to stand alone while leaving the audience wanting more

- Pad the audience by bringing a few friends or loved ones for support and to laugh when appropriate

- Begin by telling a joke to help both you and the audience relax

- If you have time, work in a personal story relating to your writing or a funny story in general

- Don't go over your allotted time, especially if you are on a panel and someone comes after you

---

54. Prum, 2001.

Author Pages

In addition to your website, blog or social media pages, you can add your profile to two popular sites: GoodReads Author Program and Amazon Author Central. Let's take a look at what each program offers.

Goodreads author program

The Goodreads program is a free tool authors can use to promote their book(s) and reach new readers. Both new and established writers use the service. You can create a profile and share as much or as little information as you like.

You can add your picture and bio, write a blog, or share a list of your favorite books or a book you have recently read. You can generate buzz for upcoming events and share excerpts from your book. You can also talk about current writing projects or post videos.

If you sell your book on the major retail sites like Amazon.com or BN.com, your book is probably already in Goodreads database — You just have to claim your page.

The service also offers many promotional tools for publicizing your book(s):

- Advertise your book through the Goodreads community

- Participate in book giveaways

- Join discussions through your profile page or in other forums for your book

How to join

If you have a Goodreads account, sign in. If not, you can sign up for a new account in minutes.

Once you are signed in, search for yourself. If your book is listed, click on your name, which should be listed below the title of your book. If you don't see your name, hold on, I'll tell you how to join in shortly. But for now, let's assume you found your book.

When you click on your name a profile page opens up. This page should have your name at the top and "author profile" located to the right of your name. Next, scroll down and click on the "Is this you?" link to join the program. It may take a few days to process your request. When approved, you'll receive an email confirmation with further instructions on how to manage your page.

Who can join

The program is for both published authors or those working on a book. You can create your profile and begin creating buzz even before you're published.

The program accepts both self-published and traditionally-published authors. You can manually add your book to the database. Once completed, you can then go back and follow the above steps that allow you to claim your profile and join the program.

Amazon author central

Your author page on Amazon.com is where readers can connect and learn more about you. You can include your bio, photos, blog, videos, and more.

How to join

To get started set up an account at www.authorcentral.amazon.com by clicking the "Join Now" button. You can use your Amazon.com customer account to sign up or create a new one if you don't have an account.

Next, find your book and link it to your account. You can then start customizing your page by adding a bio, photos, adding event information, and so on.

Once you sign up for Author Central, it may take a few days before your page appears on Amazon.com's website. Once your page is live, any updates will appear on your page within 24 hours.

Building your platform takes a lot of time and effort but if done successfully, you can establish yourself (and your brand) as a serious writer. This chapter has provided you with ideas on how to build your platform. Now it's up to you to take this advice and create your brand.

Conclusion

The decision to join the community of published writers should not be taken lightly. As you have learned from this guide, writing is hard work. I hope you have also learned that the rewards from living the writing life far outweigh the hard work you have to put in to see your name in print.

Someone asked me what career path I would I take if I could no longer make a living as a writer. That's an interesting question. I can't think of another job I would want to do besides writing. I wake up each day thinking about writing, and writing is usually the last thing I think about before I close my eyes. It is as much a part of my life as my own breath.

I congratulate you on your decision to join the writing community. Kudos for taking the first step by reading this guide. Your next move is to take the information and use it so that you can find publishing success.

Welcome to the great community of writers. Good luck with your writing projects.

Appendix A: *Additional Resources*

Books on Writing

King, Stephen. *On Writing: A Memoir of the Craft*

Browne, Renni & King, Dave. *Self-editing for Fiction Writers: How to Edit Yourself into Print*

James-Enger, Kelly. *Six-Figure Freelancing: The Writer's Guide to Making More Money*

Masello, Robert. *Robert's Rule of Writing: 101 Unconventional Lessons Every Writer Needs to Know*

Lyon, Elizabeth. *A Writer's Guide to Nonfiction*

Ragland, Margit. *Get a Freelance Life*

Formichelli, Linda & Diana Burrell. *The Renegade Writers Query Letters that Rock*

Daugherty, Greg. *You Can Write for Magazines*

Strunk, William & White, E.B. *The Elements of Style*

Rozell, Ron. Write Great Fiction: Description & Setting

Kempton, Gloria. *Write Great Fiction: Dialogue*

Bell, James Scott. *Write Great Fiction: Plot & Structure*

Bell, James Scott. *Write Great Fiction: Revision & Self-editing*

Kress, Nancy. *Write Great Fiction: Characters, Emotion, & Viewpoint*

Writer's Digest Annual Market Guides:

   Writer's Market

   Children's Writer & Illustrator's Market

   Novel & Short Story Writer's Market

   Poet's Market

Bickham, Jack. *Writing the Short Story*

Wood, Monica. *The Pocket Muse: Ideas & Inspiration for Writing*

Reeves, Judy. *A Creative Writer's Kit*

Ross, Marilyn & Collier, Sue. *The Complete Guide to Self-Publishing*

Sambuchino, Chuck. *Formatting & Submitting Your Manuscript*

The Editors of Writer's Digest Books. *The Craft & Business of Writing: Essential Tools for Writing Success*

Herman, Jeff. *Guide to Book Publishers, Editors, & Literary Agents: Who They Are, What They Want, How to Win Them Over*

Eckstut, Arielle, Sterry, David Henry. *The Essential Guide to Getting Your Book Published*

Halverson, Deborah. *Writing the Young Adult Fiction for Dummies*

Allen, Moira. *The Writer's Guide to Queries, Pitches & Proposals*

Wood, John. *How to Write Attention-Grabbing Query & Cover Letters*

Larsen, Michael. *How to Write a Book Proposal*

Websites

- **Freelance Writing Gigs:** freelancewritinggigs.com

- **American Booksellers Association:** bookweb.org

- **Wow! Women on Writing:** wow-womenonwriting.com

- **The Market List: The Online Resource for Genre Fiction Writers:** marketlist.com/

- **Adventures in YA Publishing:** adventuresinyapublishing.com

- **Freelance Writing:** freelancewriting.com

- **Highlights Foundation:** highlightsfoundation.org

- **Writerscafe.org** (Online writing community)**:** writerscafe.org

- **Problogger Jobs for Bloggers:** problogger.com/jobs

- **Jane Friedman:**janefriedman.com

- **Forward Reviews** (get your book reviewed)**:** forewordreviews.com /reviews

- **Hootsuite Social Media Manager:** hootsuite.com

- **The Purdue Online Writing Lab (OWL):** https://owl.english .purdue.edu/

Contests & Awards

- **24-Hour Short Story Contest:** Writersweekly.com

- **Boulevard Short Fiction Contest for Emerging Writers:** boulevardmagazine.org

- **The Alexander Cappon Prize for Fiction:** newletters.org/writers -wanted/writing-contests

- **The Deadly Quill Short Story Writing Contest:** deadlyquill.com

- **The Ghost Story Supernatural Fiction Award:** theghoststory.com

- **Gival Press Novel Award; Gival Press Short Story Award:** givalpress.submittable.com

- **Glimmer Train — Family Matter Contest; Fiction Open; Very Short Fiction Award for New Writers; Very Short Fiction Contest:** glimmertrain.org

- **Lorian Hemingway Short Story Competition:** shortstory competition.com

- **Tony Hillerman Prize:** wordharvest.com

- **The Iowa Short Fiction Award; John Simmons Short Fiction Award:** uiowapress.org

- **James Jones First Novel Fellowship:** wilkes.edu

- **Literal Latte Fiction Award; Short Story Contest:** literal-latte.com

- **Milkweed National Fiction Prize:** milkweed.org

- **On the Premises Contest:** onthepremises.com

- **Press 53 Award for Short Fiction:** press53.com

- **Writer's Digest Writing Competitions:** writersdigest.com/writers -digest-competitions

- **California Young Playwrights Contest:** playwrightsprojects.org /programs/contests

- **Cricket League:** cricketmagkids.com

- **Highlights for Children Fiction Contest:** highlights.com

- **Insight Writing Contest:** insightmagazine.org

- **National YoungArts Foundation:** youngarts.org

- **New Voices Award:** leeandlow.com

- **Skipping Stones Youth Honor Awards:** skippingstones.org

- **Rita Williams Young Adult Prose Prize Category:** soulmakingcontest.us

- **Paul A. Witty Outstanding Literature Award:** literacyworldwide.org

- **Yearbook Excellence Contest:** quillandscroll.org

Writing Conferences/Workshops/Classes

- **Chapter One Young Writers Conference:** chapteroneconferences.com

- **Antioch Writers' Workshop:** antiochwritersworkshop.com

- **Pacific Coast Children's Writers Whole-Novel Workshop: For Adults and Teens:** childrenswritersworkshop.com

- **Writer's Digest Conference:** writersdigest.com

- **Gotham Writer's Workshop:** writingclasses.com

- **Thriller Fest:** thrillerfest.com

- **Association of Writers & Writing Program Annual Conference:** awp.org

- **Highlights Foundation Founders Workshop:** highlightsfoundation.org

- **Alabama Writer's Conclave:** alabamawritersconclave.org

- **Iowa Summer Writing Festival:** iowasummerwritingfestival.org

- **National Writer's Association Foundation Conference:** nationalwriters.com

- **Words and Music Fest:** wordsandmusic.org

- **Tennessee Williams Literary Festival:** tennesseewilliams.net

- **Books-in-Progress Conference:** carnegiecenterlex.org/

- **Coursera:** coursera.com

- **Writer's Digest University Online Writing Classes:** writersonlineworkshops.com/

Professional Organizations

- **Mystery Writers of America:** mysterywriters.org

- **Academy of American Poets:** poets.org

- **American Crime Writer's League:** acwl.org

- **Horror Writers Association:** horror.org

- **Poetry Society of America:** poetrysocietyofamerica.org

- **Romance Writers of American:** rwa.org

- **Science Fiction and Fantasy Writers of America:** sfwa.org

- **The Author's Guild:** authorsguild.org

- **National Writer's Association:** nationalwriters.com

- **National Writers Union:** nwa.org

Glossary

Adversity: Unfavorable conditions or circumstances.

Age-restrictive: Limited to an individual who is above or below a particular age.

Ambiguous: Vague or unclear.

Authentic: Real, believable.

Book proposal: A marketing tool used by writers to sell their non-fiction book ideas to publishers.

Chronologically: Arranged in the order it happened.

Coming of Age Stories: The transition period when a young person becomes an adult.

Conglomerate: A large corporation made up of smaller companies.

Copyright: The legal right to a body of work.

Demographics: A segment of a population or group of people based on shared characteristics.

Doomsday: A disastrous event.

Espionage: The process of spying on your enemy, typically done by the government.

Expounds: To explain in detail.

Fatalistic: The belief that the outcome of an event is predetermined and cannot be changed.

Fiction: Stories that are not real.

Forge: To move ahead.

Freelancer: A person who sells his services instead of working for a salary to one employer.

Genre: A category of literary work.

Gratification: A feeling of satisfaction.

Hallmark: Typical of something.

Hybrid: A blending of two different types.

Imprint: A segment of a publishing company that markets to a specific group of readers.

Infringement: A violation of a law.

Legion: A group of people.

Mocktail: A non-alcoholic mixed drink (cocktail).

Narrative summary: A recounting of the main events in a story.

Nefarious: Evil or wicked.

Niche: A specialized market segment.

Ominous: Gloomy.

Pilfer: To steal.

Podcasting: Distributing an audio file over the Internet.

Protagonist: The hero of a story.

Public domain: Work that is no longer under copyright protection.

Red Herring: A deliberate misleading clue.

Reflowable: Electronic document that adapts to fit the screen of the device it is read on.

Repartee: Quick and witty talk or banter.

Scrutinize: To take a close look at something.

Sleuth: A detective; someone who solves a crime or mystery.

Sluggish: Slow; below the normal rates.

Stagnant: Not flowing.

Sub-genre: A subdivision of a larger genre.

Subsidiary rights: The right to publish an original work in different formats.

Synopsis: A summary of a novel.

Thwart: To stop from happening

Vanity press: A publishing house that charges writers for publishing their work.

Wordsmith: A skilled writer.

Working Title: The title an author chooses will writing their book. The publisher generally has the last word on the final title.

Writer in residence: An accomplished writer who holds a temporary position in a university setting. The writer typically gives readings and offers insights to students interested in writing careers.

Writer's Block: A temporary inability to complete a literary work in progress or create new work.

Bibliography

Chapter 1

"February 2016 Author Earnings Report: Amazon's Ebook, Print, and Audio Sales." *Authorearnings*.com. Author Earnings. 8 Feb. 2016. Web. 23 Jan. 2017.

"Flavia Bujor." *Goodreads.com*. Goodreads. Web. 10 Dec. 2016.

Atwater-Rhodes, Amelia. "About the Author." *Atwaterrhodes.com*. Amelia Atwater-Rhodes, Web. 10 Dec. 2016.

Best-Sellers Initially Rejected. Litrejections.com. Web. 08 Nov. 2016.

Eckstut, Arielle, and David Sterry. *The Essential Guide to Getting Your Book Published: How to Write It, Sell It, and Market It- Successfully!* New York: Workman Pub., 2010. 6. Print.

Goldberg, Natalie. *Writing Down the Bones: Freeing the Writer Within.* Boston: Shambhala, 1986. 101, 102. Print.

Levine, Gail Carson. *Writer to Writer: From Think to Ink.* New York: Harper, An Imprint of HarperCollins Publisher, 2015. 7. Print.

Myers, Walter Dean. *Just Write: Here's How.* New York: Collins, 2012. 17. Print.

Woolf, Virginia. *A Room of One's Own.* Harcourt, 1929. 4. Print.

Chapter 2

"Best Book Titles." Goodreads.com. Web. 15 Nov. 2016.

"Copyright in General (FAQ)." *U.S. Copyright Office.* Web. 16 Nov. 2016.

"Definition of Nonfiction." *Merriam-Webster.com.* Merriam-Webster. Web. 10 Nov. 2016.

"Frequently Asked Questions". *StephenKing.com.* Web. 14 Nov. 2016.

"Historical Fiction Books." *Goodreads.com.* Goodreads Inc. Web. 09 Nov. 2016.

"Julie Powell." Biography.com. A&E Networks Television, 08 July 2014. Web. 06 Dec. 2016.

"New Adult Books." *Goodreads.com.* Goodreads Inc. Web. 09 Nov. 2016.

"Suspense Books." *Goodreads.com.* Goodreads Inc. Web. 09 Nov. 2016.

"The Definition of Copyright." *Merriam-Webster.com.* Web. 16 Nov. 2016.

"The Definition of Freelance." *Dictionary.com.* Web. 16 Nov. 2016.

"The Definition of Genre." *Dictionary.com.* Web. 09 Nov. 2016.

"The Definition of Subgenre." *Dictionary.com.* Web. 09 Nov. 2016.

"The Romance Genre" Romance Writers of America. Web. 09 Nov. 2016.

"Thriller Books." *Goodreads.com.* Goodreads Inc. Web. 09 Nov. 2016.

"What Is Horror Fiction?" Horror Writers Association. Web. 09 Nov. 2016.

Eckstut, Arielle, and David Sterry. *The Essential Guide to Getting Your Book Published: How to Write It, Sell It, and Market It-- Successfully!* New York: Workman Pub., 2010. 64, 152 292. Print.

Fletcher, Ralph. "Writing Masters: Keeping A Writer's Notebook." *Heine-mann.com*. Houghton, Mifflin, Harcourt, 23 Feb. 2015. Web. 12 Nov. 2016.

Goldberg, Natalie. *Writing down the Bones: Freeing the Writer within*. Boston: Shambhala, 1986. 6. Print.

King, Stephen. *On Writing: 10th Anniversary Edition*. New York, New York: Simon & Schuster, 2010. 215-20. Print.

Masello, Robert. *Robert's Rules of Writing: 101 Unconventional Lessons Every Writer Needs to Know*. Cincinnati, OH: Writer's Digest, 2005. Rule 3. Print.

Masello, Robert. *Robert's Rules of Writing: 101 Unconventional Lessons Every Writer Needs to Know*. Cincinnati, OH: Writer's Digest, 2005. Rule 51. Print.

Myers, Walter Dean. *Just Write: Here's How*. New York: Collins, 2012. 115, 117-118. Print.

Tedesco, Anthony. "Overcoming Writer's Block." *The Craft & Business of Writing: Essential Tools for Writing Success*. Cincinnati, OH: Writer's Digest, 2008. 25-28. Print.

The First Line Literary Journal: It All Starts the Same But. . . . Blue Cubicle Press, LLC, Web. 14 Nov. 2016.

Vaughn, Michael J. "Creative Lollygagging." *Writer's Digest* Oct.-Nov. 2006: 45, 99. Print.

Writer's Encyclopedia. Cincinnati, OH: Writer's Digest, 1996. 223, 337, 386, 378, 448, 396, 449, 484. Print.

Chapter 3

"Alexandra Adornetto." *MacMillan*. Web. 07 Dec. 2016.

"Alexandra Adornetto." *Goodreads*. Web. 07 Dec. 2016.

"Espresso Book Machine." *On Demand Books*. On Demand Books. Web. 07 Dec. 2016.

"Former Self-Pub Winner Lands Book Contract." Writer's Digest June 2008: 14. Print.

"John Hopkins University Press: History." John Hopkins University Press. Web. 21 Nov. 2016.

Bourne, Michael. "All in the Family." Poets & Writers Nov.-Dec. 2012: 68-77. Print.

Browne, Renni, and Dave King. *Self-editing for Fiction Writers: How to Edit Yourself into Print*. New York: Harper Resource, 2004. 8, 10, 19, 84. Print.

Eckstut, Arielle, and David Sterry. *The Essential Guide to Getting Your Book Published: How to Write It, Sell It, and Market It- Successfully!* New York: Workman Pub., 2010. 271. Print.

Gibson, Tanya Egan. "10 Things Your Freelance Editor Might Not Tell You- But Should." *Writer's Digest* May-June 2013: 27-30. Web.

Goldberg, Natalie. *Writing Down the Bones: Freeing the Writer Within*. Boston: Shambhala, 1986. 70. Print.

Humphrey, Elizabeth King. "Running on Heart." The Writer 124.9 (2011): 28-29. Web.

Levine, Mark. *The Fine Print of Self-publishing: Everything You Need to Know about the Costs, Contracts & Process of Self-publishing*. Minneapolis, MN: Bascom Hill Group, 2011. 2. Print.

Pfanner, Eric, and Amy Chozick. "Random House and Penguin Merger Creates Global Giant." The New York Times. The New York Times, 29 Oct. 2012. Web. 05 Dec. 2016.

Chapter 4

"The Definition of Glyph." *En.Oxforddictionaries.com*. Web. 07 Jan. 2017.

Greenfield, Jeremy. "What Writers Need to Know About the E-book Market." Writer's Digest Feb. 2014: 21-25. Print.

Zickuhr, Kathryn, and Lee Rainie. "E-Reading Rises as Device Ownership Jumps." *Pew Research Center: Internet, Science & Tech*. Pew Research Center, 16 Jan. 2014. Web. 05 Jan. 2017.

Chapter 5

"Association of Authors' Representatives, Inc." *Association of Authors' Representatives, Inc.* AAR, Inc. Web. 13 Jan. 2017.

"Subsidiary Rights." *Dictionary.com*. Dictionary.com. Web. 12 Jan. 2017.

Eckstut, Arielle, and David Sterry. *The Essential Guide to Getting Your Book Published: How to Write It, Sell It, and Market It- Successfully!* New York: Workman Pub., 2010. 105-106. Print.

Katzenberger, Lisa. "Pitch Agents Through Twitter." *Children's Writer's & Illustrator's Market 2017*. Ed. Chuck Sambuchino and Nancy Parish. Cincinnati, OH: Writer's Digest, 2016. 27-31. Print.

Sambuchino, Chuck and Haney, Hannah. "New Agent Spotlights: Learn About New Reps Seeking Clients." *Children's Writer's & Illustrator's Market 2017*. Ed. Chuck Sambuchino and Nancy Parish. Cincinnati, OH: Writer's Digest, 2016. 27-31. Print.

Tedesco, Anthony. "Overcoming Writer's Block." *The Craft & Business of Writing: Essential Tools for Writing Success.* Cincinnati, OH: Writer's Digest, 2008. 144-148. Print.

Chapter 6

"Before Your First Sale." *Writer's Market 2017.* Ed. Robert Lee Brewer. Cincinnati, OH: Writer's Digest, 2016. 8-14. Print.

"Query Letter Clinic." *Writer's Market 2017.* Ed. Robert Lee Brewer. Cincinnati, OH: Writer's Digest, 2016. 15-25. Print.

Camenson, Blythe, and Marsha J. Cook. "The Rock-Solid Submission Package." *Writing Basics: A Beginner's Guide to Writing* (2006): 54-58. Print.

Herman, Jeff & Deborah. "Write the Perfect Query Letter." *Jeff Herman's Guide to Book Publishers, Editors & Literary Agents: Who They Are, What They Want, How to Win Them over.* Jeff Herman. Novato, CA: New World Library, 2016. 19-24. Print.

Herman, Jeff. "The Knockout Nonfiction Book Proposal." *Jeff Herman's Guide to Book Publishers, Editors & Literary Agents: Who They Are, What They Want, How to Win Them over.* Novato, CA: New World Library, 2016. 31-36. Print.

Hodges, SJ. "Landing the Six-Figure Deal: What Makes Your Proposal Hot." *Writer's Market 2017.* Ed. Robert Lee Brewer. Cincinnati, OH: Writer's Digest, 2016. 30-35. Print.

Jennings, Holly. "5 Reasons Queries Get Rejected." *Children's Writer's & Illustrator's Market 2017.* Ed. Chuck Sambuchino and Nancy Parish. Cincinnati, OH: Writer's Digest, 2016. 43-48. Print.

Rock, Maya. "The Do's and Don'ts of Agent Queries". *The Writer* (April 2008): 40-41. Print.

Chapter 7

Buckham, Mary. "8 Elements To Amplify Your Author Brand." *Novel & Short Story Writer's Market 2017:* . Ed. Rachel Randall. Cincinnati, OH: Writer's Digest, 2016. 81-86. Print.

Campbell, Carolyn. "Book Signings Add Up to Book Sales." *The Writer* (August 2006): 40-41. Print.

Davidson, MaryJanice. "A Friendly Chat Pays Dividends." *The Writer* (April 2002): 17-19. Print.

Demarco-Barrett, Barbara. "Build Your Website." *Writer's Yearbook 2007* (2007): 56-59. Print.

DiSilverio, Laura. "Pinterest is Worth a Thousand Words." *Writer's Digest* (September 2012): 10-11. Print.

Formichelli, Linda. "The Anatomy of a Writer's Website." *Writer's Digest* (October 2008): 51-55. Print.

Fry, Patricia. "7 Ways to Use Your Website to Sell Books." *The Writer* (January 2012): 29-30. Print.

Hendrickson, Nancy. "Use Podcasts to Promote Your Book." *The Writer* (November 2007): 36. Print.

Konraith, J.A. "Book-Signing Success. "*Writer's Digest* (June 2007): 48-53. Print.

Prum, Deborah. "How to Give a Good Reading." *The Writer* (May 2001): 34-36. Print.

Rider, Karen. "Make Your Homepage POP: Follow These Basic Principles to Boost Your Web Traffic." *The Writer* (September 2012): 26-27. Print.

Rosenberg, Gigi. "Marketing: Give a Good Reading. "*Writer's Digest* (October 2007): 52-57. Print.

Sanders, Leslie Lee. How to Develop an Effective Author Brand." *Writer's Market 2017*. Ed. Robert Lee Brewer. Cincinnati, OH: Writer's Digest, 2016. 69-73. Print.

Sims, Elizabeth. "Going Public: How to Ace Readings, Singings, Interviews & More." Wr*iter's Digest* (September 2013): 26-29. Print.

Sundblad, Donna. "Moveable Feasts Serve up Book-Promotion Possibilities." *The Writer* (April 2008): 12-14. Print.

The *Writer's Digest* Staff. "A Writer's Guide to Social Networking. "*Writer's Digest (*May/June 2009): 40-41. Print.

Index

A

Adventure 6, 43, 51, 91, 100
Advertising 95, 192
Agency 109, 153
Artwork 94
Author Central 9, 201, 203
Author platform 9, 149, 159, 176, 177

B

Bibliography 10, 217
Biography 6, 51, 52, 218
Blog 20, 60, 80-82, 101, 150, 177, 183, 184, 201, 203
Book copy 133, 138
Book cover 110, 133
Book reading 189, 195
Book signings 9, 21, 185, 189, 193-195, 223
Book tours 95
Book trailer 174, 187

C

Children's book 15, 103-105
CIP 2, 94
Contract 7, 20, 32, 67, 86, 92-97, 100, 103, 142, 143, 148, 156-159, 220
Contests 7, 10, 21, 69, 72, 84, 85, 101, 107, 166, 176, 209, 210
Copy editing 109
Copyright 2, 7, 8, 70, 77, 85, 86, 94, 96, 108, 110, 134, 213, 215, 218
Cover letter 84, 162
CreateSpace 7, 104, 108-110, 113, 121, 127
Crime 6, 40, 41, 53, 212, 215

D

Deadline 32, 33, 82
Dialogue 51, 60, 63, 64, 88, 207
Digital rights management (DRM) 8, 134, 135

Distribution 95, 102, 109, 110, 118, 119, 125, 128

Draft 32, 67, 68, 72, 75, 89, 90, 103, 104, 115, 172

E

E-book 1, 2, 8, 19, 48, 104, 111, 117-127, 130-134, 136, 137, 173, 221

E-publish 8, 117

Editor 7, 13, 26, 29, 32, 33, 76, 82, 85, 86, 94, 99, 109, 114, 115, 126, 127, 143, 145, 150, 161, 163-169, 171, 173-178, 183, 184, 188, 220

Events 11, 42, 45-47, 72, 112, 149, 150, 167, 168, 182, 183, 185, 188, 189, 197, 198, 201, 214

F

Facebook 9, 11, 146, 152, 178, 182, 185, 186

Fantasy 6, 15, 39, 41, 43, 100, 212

Fiction 5, 6, 17, 34, 38, 40, 42-44, 51, 78, 84, 87, 88, 92, 145, 153, 183, 207-212, 214, 218, 220

Film rights 93

Formatting 8, 19, 108, 122, 127, 131, 132, 208

Freelancing 7, 82, 98, 207

G

Genre 5, 18, 37-39, 43, 44, 51, 54, 59, 66, 67, 84, 104, 105, 138, 143, 153, 155, 162, 165, 168, 183, 185, 209, 214, 215, 218

Goodreads 9, 40, 42, 43, 79, 201, 202, 217, 218, 220

Grammar 94, 109

H

Historical 6, 39, 42, 47, 83, 87, 218

Hook 56, 78, 133, 165, 169

Horror 6, 39, 43, 69, 115, 189, 212, 218

How-to 6, 47, 48

I

Illustrator 103, 104, 157, 208, 221, 222

Imprint 99, 100, 114, 127, 214, 217

J

Journal 6, 17, 60, 61, 219

K

Kindle 122, 124, 125, 127, 133, 136

L

Library of Congress Control Number 94

Literary agent 8, 19, 35, 91, 104, 105, 141, 142, 147, 149, 150, 152
Lulu 7, 110, 111

M
Magazines 82, 95, 207
Manuscript 5, 18-20, 24-27, 30, 32-35, 37, 67, 75, 76, 78, 84, 86, 88, 89, 91-95, 97, 101, 104, 107, 114, 115, 125-129, 131, 132, 138, 139, 141-143, 145, 147, 149, 157-159, 161-164, 166-169, 176, 208
Marketing 44-46, 93-95, 102, 104, 106, 107, 111, 120, 128, 143, 148, 171, 174, 189, 213, 224
Memoir 6, 52, 53, 75, 187, 207
Mystery 6, 41, 65, 72, 212, 215

N
Narrative nonfiction 51
Newspaper 83, 166
National novel writing month (NaNoWriMo) 7, 72
Nonfiction 6, 46, 47, 51, 77, 80, 153, 161, 169, 187, 207, 218, 222
Novel 7, 14, 38, 39, 41-43, 51, 72, 73, 87, 114, 117, 138, 147,

161, 163, 166-168, 177, 179, 208, 210, 215, 223

P
Paperback 111
Payment 109, 125
Pictures 50, 70, 187
Pitch Package 8, 19, 145, 148, 157, 161, 162, 176, 194
Poetry 26, 55, 85, 103, 144, 212
Portfolio 103, 183
Pricing 8, 119, 137, 139
Print-on-demand (POD) 107
Promotion 93, 104, 105, 145
Protagonist 43, 168, 214

Q
Qualifications 166
Query letter 9, 145, 159, 161, 163-165, 167, 222

R
Revising 7, 19, 86, 89
Romance 5, 37-39, 41, 43, 59, 100, 145, 212, 218
Royalties 94, 97, 104, 105, 108, 110, 113, 128

S
Sample chapters 91, 92, 145, 147, 161, 169, 171, 172, 176
Science Fiction 6, 17, 40, 87, 212

Self-help 6, 47-49

Self-publishing 13, 26, 93, 98, 103, 104, 106-108, 113, 121, 125, 127, 131, 133, 136, 144, 146, 208, 220

SmashWords 127-130

Social Media 74, 101, 104, 105, 139, 146, 152, 155, 180, 181, 186-188, 192, 201, 209

Social networking 9, 21, 184, 185, 224

Subsidiary rights 148, 215, 221

Subtitle 78

Synopsis 9, 145, 147, 161, 167-169, 182, 215

T

Table of Contents 5, 172, 173, 175

The Author's Guild 212

Thriller 6, 39, 41, 42, 169, 211, 218

Tone 34, 169, 172, 179, 190

Travel Guides 6, 47, 49, 50

Travelogues 6, 51

True crime 6, 53

Twitter 9, 44, 45, 83, 152, 182, 185, 221

U

University Press 101, 144, 220

V

Vanity press 112, 113, 215

Voice 88, 89, 115, 147, 163, 168, 169, 172, 179, 199

W

Western 42

Writing Group 6, 19, 29, 56-58, 60, 115

Y

Youtube 9, 20, 174, 177, 188, 189

About the Author

Myra Faye Turner is a freelance writer and author of *Poems in Poetry*, a collection of her best poetry and *The Young Adult's Guide to Identity Theft: A Step-by-Step Guide to Stopping Scammers* (Atlantic Publishing). She spends most of her day writing or dreaming about writing. She lives in New Orleans with her teenaged son, Tyler.